I0670924

Glimpses of Wilderness

Lee Ann Ward

The characters and events in this book are fictitious. Any similarity to real persons, living or dead, places, or events is coincidental and not intended by the author.

If you purchase this book without a cover you should be aware that this book may have been stolen property and reported as "unsold and destroyed" to the publisher. In such case the author has not received any payment for this "stripped book."

Glimpses of Wilderness
Copyright © 2017 Lee Ann Ward
All rights reserved.

ISBN: (ebook) 978-1-945910-44-9
(print) 978-1-945910-81-4

Inkspell Publishing
5764 Woodbine Ave.
Pinckney, MI 48169

Edited By Rie Langdon
Cover art By Najla Qamber

This book, or parts thereof, may not be reproduced in any form without permission. The copying, scanning, uploading, and distribution of this book via the internet or via any other means without the permission of the publisher is illegal and punishable by law. Please purchase only authorized electronic or print editions, and do not participate in or encourage piracy of copyrighted materials. Your support of the author's rights is appreciated.

DEDICATION

To Joyce Scarbrough, my best friend and author whose wonderful book was the inspiration for GLIMPSES. Had it not been for Mickey and Jeana, my Robert and Anna would have never been realized. Thank you for writing TRUE BLUE FOREVER and reminding me what timeless love feels like.

Joyce, this one is yours.

Our truest life is when we are in dreams awake.——Henry David Thoreau

CHAPTER 1

Drip. Drip.

If Mom were herself, she'd scream for me to turn the handle down tighter—stop the infernal torture of water collecting in the sink, one irrelevant drop at a time. But she's not herself. She's drunk. *Again.* Seventeen years later and she still misses them, can describe the smell of my sister's hair like she'd just braided it for her yesterday. Earthy, like rain mingled with honeysuckle. And long, to her waist. My hair's never been that long. Well, at least not in this lifetime.

Drip. Drip.

I can handle her talking about Paige—that was my sister's name, Paige Marie Berkeley. But when she talks about my dad, the one who never held me, hugged me, or even loved me… How could he? He never even knew I existed. When it happened, my dad had just picked up my eight-year-old sister from ballet class and was on his way to a restaurant to meet Mom. She was going to tell them both about me, the three-month-happily-baking fetus in her belly, when the semi blindsided Dad's Acura. Never knew

3

what hit them. Mom was still in the restaurant when she got the call.

It was a sushi restaurant.

We never eat sushi.

Drip. Drip. Thud.

She's missed the couch, again…probably slumped near the coffee table. I twist the handle for the cold water so tight it pinches my palm and the drips fade away.

"There's my girl," Mom says when my feet are three inches from her face. "Be a sweetheart and help me to the couch."

"How about your bed?" I ask. "It's one in the morning." When she doesn't protest, I drape her limp arm around my neck and lead her to the hallway. A combo of sweat and pee assaults my nose, but I can't move a hand to cover it or she'll fall. She's already fallen hard enough tonight, too hard for me to let go.

"You would have loved them, Anna," she mutters.

"I know," I say. It's what I always say.

"My Michael was so handsome. Best looking guy in…well…anywhere." She laughs and I turn my face from hers to avoid the breath that's worse than her B.O. Then the laughter turns to sobs. "He was so funny too, Anna. And my Paige. Oh, my beautiful Paige."

When she's finally in bed, I sit on the edge and roll her to the middle. "There you go, Mom. You'll be okay." Before I can stand, she sits up and cups my face.

"Why don't you look like him? You're supposed to look like him. Your sister looked exactly like him, hair so blond—"

It was almost white, I mouth with her, but don't say it.

Mom's eyes furiously scan my face like she's looking for evidence, proof that I'm part of the perfect world that was once hers before I came along. Then she does the one thing that calms her every single time this plays out. She looks past my ashy brown hair and tanned skin and stares me dead in the eyes.

"Oh, my Michael. There he is…those green eyes."

"A perfect match," we say in unison, and she lies down to sleep it off.

I close her door, careful not to bang it on the loose hinges, and head to my own room again. I hate it when she does this, but blaming her for missing them would make me the biggest hypocrite on the planet. After all, I'm missing someone, too.

And I haven't seen him in over two hundred years.

***

I was crazy tired before Mom almost collided with the coffee table. I'm always afraid she'll roll out of bed or choke on her own vomit when she has nights like this. She never has, but I worry about it anyway. I look at my phone again. 3:00 a.m. Thank God it's Saturday, but I'm on schedule to volunteer at the nursing home at nine, and I can't be late. I'm too close to winning the Sunshine Merit Scholarship to let something like no sleep land me a demerit. I purposely hold my eyes open for as long as I can, trying to make them sting enough that I'll fall asleep.

"Get a grip, Anna," I whisper when all the forced staring earns me is burning eyes. I bury the side of my face deeper into the feather pillow. Maybe William's awake… Nope. No way I'm texting him now. God, he'd love that. I touch Maggie's name instead.

I'm gonna be sooo
dead tomorrow.

Text delivered, not read. She's asleep. *Lucky her.* I find the sweet spot on my pillow when I flip it, and take a few deep breaths, attempting to shut off my racing brain. It does feel good to close my eyes…

I don't spot him straight away. Robert's body is tiny compared to the incredible height and mass of trees in the distance. I wipe my hands on a stained apron. I wish I had a clean one, but the wash is days old and the baby's sick, so it will wait. At least I have a decent supper over the flame, and my husband isn't particular about food. It's one of the things I love about him.

I check my reflection in a tin plate when I hear his boots on the porch, and tuck a few loose strands of hair behind one ear. I pinch my cheeks for pinkness then collect some bowls for the rabbit stew.

"Anna," Robert says when the door unlatches. "How's the little one?"

"She's sleeping but less feverish."

"And Robert Jr.?"

"Still no signs of sickness with him. I think the worst is over."

"That's good," Robert replies. "Come here. I have something to show you."

He drops the leather sack in his hands when I reach him and scoops me into his arms. When his mouth covers mine, it's like the first breath I've taken since he left the cabin that morning. I breathe in the flannel and earth still clinging to his dusting of beard, his hands grasping my hips, gathering the fabric covering them like he's clinging for life. A hand slides to my cheek and he cups it, nudging my lips open as his kiss softens.

"I've missed you," he whispers into my hair.

"But it's only been since the morn—"

"And that's too long." He pulls my face forward and kisses my forehead. "Now sit. I really do have something to show you."

I'm barely in the chair when Robert sets a coin pouch in front of me. "Open it."

I dump the coins out and lose my breath. "These aren't shillings...they're crowns! But how?" I do a mental count. Nine crowns total. "Robert, where did you get these?"

"Mr. Besson liked the table I made for him so much that he agreed to sell my furniture in his general store. He gave me the crowns for material costs." Robert's eyes light up so much they barely resemble the deep mahogany hue I know them to be. "Do you know what this means, Anna? A whole new life for us, that's what. And look." He pulls a paper from his shirt pocket. "I signed a document of accord with him too, for a whole year."

I scan the paper, one word and a string of numbers striking me harder than a blow to the face:

September 23, 1805.

My bedroom's still dark when a car horn jars me awake. I don't bother with the time. The sun isn't up yet. Tears sting my eyes. *September 23, 1805.* I was right—it *has* been over two hundred years.

I've had normal dreams before, ones about falling or flying, and some about being in a house I don't recognize or having strange people chase me. I even dreamed about starting the first day of sixth grade totally naked, but that was then. I don't dream anymore...not in five years. No floating, no flying, no nightmares about my dad's car crashing or my sister's tiny face vanishing in a window of red. No, not anymore.

Now when I sleep I fall into an expanse of frozen wilderness, the other life I've lived...the one I lived with him.

CHAPTER 2

I'm in the door five minutes before my shift starts. Even though I'm technically not late, I hate signing in, and only having a couple of minutes to read the notes I'm given about the elderly residents, like who had a great night, or who flung scrambled eggs at New York. Yes, that's one of the nurses' names: New York. Even though I love all the old people here, it always takes some deep breathing to mentally prepare for the morning ahead. Love's hard, and grump-bag Mr. Nathan is the first name on my clipboard. Yeah, love's freakin' brutal.

I've volunteered as a Sunshine Warrior at the Greater Tuscaloosa Convalescent Home since my freshman year with one goal in mind—the Sunshine Merit Scholarship. A high school senior is awarded a ten-thousand-dollar college scholarship from the organization that founded the Warriors, and this is my year. Only two seniors are demerit free, and I'm one of them. The other is a guy named Dustin Mears. But Dustin became a volunteer his sophomore year, so as long as I stay demerit-less, the money's mine. I got this.

My grades are fine, but I suck at numbers. With straight Bs in math, I'll still qualify for some kind of academic scholarship too, but I'll never be given a godawful amount of money like the A-listers. Those numbers I *don't* have a problem with. So I need the Sunshine Warriors, need my own money for school, so my mom can hang on to some of hers. Dad left a hefty life insurance policy behind when he died, and thank goodness Mom's good with money. But rehab ain't cheap, and she needs to check back in soon. We both know it. She's worse now than any of the other times she's relapsed. She's the kind of broken that shows, like when you superglue something along a perfect crack and just one tiny chip is missing. It'll never be truly fixed, but it's still good, still serves a purpose. I don't need Mom perfect, I just need her to be good again.

"Morning, Mr. Nathan," I announce before pulling on the door to his room. The soft humming that greets me when I step inside is a welcome sound. Thank God he's sleeping. He's usually way too cranky in the mornings to deal with, anyway. I'll come back later.

And now I can go see Rose.

I stop at her door before going inside. She usually whistles when she's alone, but quits the moment she thinks someone's listening. Not sure why, though. She's phenomenal at it. All I ever managed in the whistling arena added up to spitting through my teeth.

"Rose, hello-hello," I say when I'm in the door.

"There's my Anna," she replies. "How's your week been, dear?"

"Okay. A little rough, but okay."

"Has the drinking gotten worse?"

It's funny. I've always been so closed off when it comes to my life. I've been friends with Maggie since fifth grade, but I've never told her about Mom's drinking problem. Honestly, I can count on one hand the times Maggie's spent the night at my house. But it's different with Rose. She's eighty-eight years old and my best friend in the world.

"Yeah," I say. "It was horrible last night. She fell again.

Her head missed the coffee table by an inch, thank God, but she was okay once I got her in bed. She was still sleeping it off when I left this morning."

Rose tugs at the strand of pearls dangling from her bony neck. She looks like an aging, classic film star. She's thin, but a *good* thin, not the *sickly old people* thin. She wears her silver hair clipped up in a loose bun with wispy curls teasing her face. Her shirts are always silky, button-front, and her skirts are straight and to the ankle. Her costume jewelry is chunky and oversized, including the rings she balances on her long, skinny fingers—the embodiment of elegance.

"And how much sleep did *you* get last night?" Rose asks.

I sit in the chair beside her. "Not much."

"You know she needs professional help again, right?" Rose's eyes search mine. "You can't do this alone."

"I know, and we actually talk about it when she's sober. She doesn't drink as much during the week because she can't miss work. But the weekends…" I look at my feet this time. "The weekends are rough."

Rose wraps an arm around my shoulders. "I'm so sorry, dear. So, when do you think she'll check into rehab again?"

"Her vacation time starts over again next month. She said something about putting in for a few weeks then. I just hope they give it to her without much argument. The bank she works in is usually pretty cool, though."

"Well, that's good."

"Something else happened last night, though," I say, "and it was actually kind of amazing."

Rose scoots forward like her hearing aid's malfunctioning. "So tell me all about it."

"I had another dream about Robert."

Only two people in the world know about my past life memories: my mom and Rose. But over the past couple of years, Rose has become my main confidante. Mom gets way too weirded out when I talk about it.

11

"What did you see?"

"Robert and our children. He came home with a pouch full of money from some furniture he'd made. Then he showed me a contract he'd signed, and, Rose…it had a date on it."

She slides a sweet, wrinkled hand on top of mine. "A date?"

"September 23, 1805."

A slight gasp escapes Rose's thin lips. "1805? Good heavens, child. That is something else. Truly remarkable, really. So, do you plan to research—?"

"No," I cut in. "I don't really have any desire to research it. I don't know, Rose, but it's just…when I'm with Robert in my dreams, it's like I'm finally home after a long journey. Every nerve in my body reacts to him. I can feel. I can move. I can breathe." I look into Rose's seeking, blue eyes. "I know it sounds crazy, but it's like I have to be asleep to feel truly awakened."

She's quiet for several seconds, no doubt allowing my words to fully register. I gather the dirty linens at the foot of her bed and toss them in the hamper.

"I hope I live another life someday," Rose says, "but I would want it to be with Ted. I miss him so much."

"I know," I say, sitting next to her again. "How long has he been gone now?"

"Gosh, it's been almost ten years now," she replies. "He held on longer than the cancer should've let him."

"I know," I say. "I remember you telling me."

"But he didn't want to leave me here all alone," she continues, like I didn't say anything at all. "We lost our Teddy a few years before that—"

"And his wife was a pain in the butt."

Rose grins. "I never said that, Anna, but I definitely wasn't her biggest fan."

"I wonder why they never had kids." I blurt out the words before realizing how intrusive they sound.

"It just wasn't in the cards, I suppose. But she

remarried a few years after my Teddy died. I do hope she's happy, wherever she is now. I guess Ted knew I'd eventually end up alone, huh?"

"You're not alone. You have me."

Rose pulls me into a hug. "I know I do, sweet girl. And that's why I want my personal belongings to go to you if something happens to me—"

"Don't talk like that. Nothing's going to happen to you."

"I know, I know. But I need to tell you this, okay?"

I nod.

"As far as money goes, I don't have any. The nursing home gets that. But there's a box in the closet. When I'm gone, that's yours. I've already informed the staff that anything you want in this room is yours too, so dispose of it however you see fit. Understand? I love you, Anna. You're like the granddaughter I never had."

I do understand, but I can't go there, can't ever think about losing Rose.

"Okay, enough grim talk," I say. "What's going on in the activities room today? Knitting? Singing? Maybe a little Zumba fitness?" I do a few hip shakes and Rose laughs.

She diverts the question. "Do you have plans with William tonight?"

"We're going to the movies," I reply, "and I'm not ashamed to admit that I can't wait to gorge myself on popcorn and Sno-Caps."

"He sounds like such a nice young man. When do I get to meet him?"

"Soon, I promise."

I've asked William a few times to come with me so he can meet Rose, but he always seems crazy busy on weekends. We've only been dating a couple of months, and I really like him, even though he moves a little faster than I want to at the moment. But Rose, she would eat that boy up with a spoon.

"Be honest," Rose says. "William just hates old-people

smell."

I crack up. "God, Rose! I can't believe you're talking about old-people smell. And by the way, you might be aging, but you don't smell like 'old people'."

"I'm not talking about me, Anna. I'm talking about you. You ever smelled yourself after you leave Mr. Nathan's room? Phew-wee."

***

As rough as yesterday was, tonight is actually shaping up to be pretty perfect. Mom felt so guilty about last night, she promised not to drink while William and I are on our date. The humidity isn't stifling like it usually is in Alabama in late August, and the sky's clear and dotted with a million stars.

"So," William asks as we walk to his car, "did you like the movie?"

"I liked being able to sit down for a couple of hours and do nothing," I say. "I haven't stopped much, lately."

"I can tell," William says. "You look tired."

"Hey…"

"I didn't mean it that way."

I tug on his arm. "Yeah, right."

He stops and pulls me closer, running a hand through my messy-but-I-don't-care hair. "I think you're the most beautiful girl in this town."

And I believe him. It's what attracted me to William in the first place. Well, that and his dark, curly hair and killer smile. The guy practically oozes sweetness. We met at a concert in the park a couple of months ago. It was my first summer outing after finishing my junior year, and Maggie had bailed on me at the last minute. So, I did what I normally don't and went alone. I spotted William helping a skeletal girl off the ground. No telling what she was high on, but he made sure she was back safely with her friends before leaving her side. It was chivalry at its finest. I'm not

14

sure if my utter loneliness was the culprit for my boldness, but I bumped into him on purpose that night, and we've been whatever we are ever since.

"So, you think I'm pretty, huh?"

William presses the words against my face. "No, I said you're beautiful." His lips trail across my forehead and cheek. It tickles, but I don't dare move. When his mouth meets mine, I lean into his body, needing more than anything to feel his closeness. His lips are soft, searching, coaxing with a tenderness that almost begs me to want him as much as he wants me. But when his hands slide from my hair to my neck, as tender as the moment is, I wince. I clasp his hands in mine and ease them away.

Confusion lines his eyes as he breaks the kiss. "Did I do something wrong?"

God, why did I do that? "No, Will. I'm sorry. It's just...I don't like for my neck to be touched. I know it sounds stupid, and I'm not sure why, but my neck hurts when it's touched. Do you think I'm weird now?"

He tries to hold in a grin, but fails. "Yes, I think you're weird." But his smile says differently. "Seriously, it's no big deal. It's not like *I vant to suck your blood.*"

"Yeah, well, the only thing that sucks is your Dracula impression."

He kisses me again before asking, "So, wanna get outta here?"

"We can go to The Spot," I say.

"Perfect."

The Spot is a wooded area near my house. I discovered it when I was eight. That day, Mom had a major hangover and I had a cold. Every time I sneezed she complained that the noise was like an axe through her skull, so I took me and my runny nose outside for some exploring. The cool thing about The Spot is that the woods there seem impossible to pass through at first, but then a small trail leads to a clearing nestled between some trees. And if you lie on the grass on a clear night, the stars are better than a planetarium. I used to call it Star-tacular, but changed the name to The Spot when I decided to share it with William.

It's hard to get a word in once we're on the highway. Will's excited about the first football game next Friday night. He's the kicker for Central High School. I go to Northridge. We've only been back in school for a week, but so far the different-school thing's no biggie. Sometimes I enjoy the buffer, and it gives us more to talk about—especially since discussing my mom's drinking and the deaths of the rest of my family isn't something I'm very comfortable sharing with Will just yet. I mean, how do you tell someone the details of something you had no part of, and yet it defines your very existence? And then there's Robert...

For the longest time, dating was something I wasn't very interested in. Everything about being in the wild with Robert and our babies consumed me, even now. The first time I dreamed of him, I was convinced it was just that, a dream. But the more it occurred, the more the memories—real memories—replaced the doubt. I know things about that time, like how to cook and sew. I know how to tend wounds and make ointments from plants. Hell, I know how I made soap back then. I remember what it felt like to make love to my husband, the man I craved more than air, what it felt like to carry and give birth to our babies, and yet here I am in this life, a seventeen-year-old virgin. I know Robert. Know us. And that's the point. I know, and I can't *unknow*.

"Hey," William says. "Well?"

I hadn't heard his question. I'd been too busy reliving my wilderness past for the umpteenth time. "I'm sorry. What?"

"Next Friday night. You're coming to my game, right?"

"Of course. I wouldn't miss it."

William's eyes shine like sunlight on glass. "Good. I was scared you'd want to go to the Northridge game."

"Well, I don't have the hots for any of the players on

Northridge. And besides, I can't wait to see how you look in those pants."

He shakes his head. "That's just wrong."

William parks on the street when we're near the woods. The flashlight app on my phone glows to life as I take Will's hand and pull him along. I always lead the way. In a few minutes we're sitting on the cool, damp grass looking at the stars. Doesn't seem like as many are out as I initially thought, but it's decent.

"So," I say as William wraps his arms around my shoulders and I lean my back into his chest, "Rose really wants to meet you in person. She probably thinks I made you up at this point."

"I know, I know," he says. "I promise I'll try to stop by there next Saturday morning, okay?"

"Okay, but I'm holding you to it."

"You know," he says, "you hound me more about meeting that sweet old lady than you do about meeting your mom."

"No I don't." *Yes I do.* I'm actually stumped for a moment, not sure what to say. I love Mom to pieces, and I want them to meet. But this has been a rough summer for us, much too rough for me to invite William into the madness just yet. "So the game Friday night," I say instead, "do I just meet you afterward or something? You know, since you'll be rock-starring it out on the field and everything."

"Sure. You can just wait by the field house after the game. That way, I can show you off to some of the guys."

"Oh I see. I'm just a pretty face to you, huh?"

He's suddenly serious. "No, Anna. I wish you could see that you're so much more than that."

William nudges me to face him and his mouth finds mine in the darkness. The kiss is slow and tender. His lips are soft and warm, and I arch my back a little when a hand tangles in my hair. He slips his other one under the hem of my sundress, hitching it up until that hand is resting on my thigh. His fingers are hot as he traces lines on my skin, but I focus on the salty taste of his mouth instead. I can feel his muscles harden through the thin fabric of his shirt. I know he wants me, and I need so much to want him too. I urge my mind to let go of Robert, to shed the misplaced guilt that keeps me living in a past that will never be again. I need William to touch me—need it more than I need air at the moment. Right now I just need to feel normal.

He nibbles my bottom lip, pulling me closer. I follow his motions, tingles teasing my stomach as I hold my breath to calm the flutters. But when his hand eases further up my thigh, dangerously close to the boyshorts I always wear under my dresses, I catch his hand.

"I'm sorry, William. I can't do this."

His breathing's still intense as he pulls back and searches my eyes. "I'm sorry, Anna. I'd never make you do anything you didn't want to." He lowers his head. "But I seem to do everything wrong with you." Then he whispers, "Everything."

He's never done *anything* wrong. I've brought every drop of awkwardness to the party when it comes to us and I know it. I wish I could get a grip—been wishing it for a while now.

"This is just moving a little too fast for me," I say. "I'm sorry"

"Fast? But we…" He shuts his mouth instead.

I don't look at him. "Can we just go to my house now?"

His voice is barely a whisper. "Yeah, sure. Whatever."

Guilt thuds my chest like a drum and I take his hands in mine. "I really am sorry, Will. Just give me a little more time. This is all just really new for me, okay?"

He nods and I squeeze his hands for reassurance and he places a short kiss on my forehead. I grab my phone and stand, shining the now illuminated flashlight app toward the trail again. My phone sounds an alert.

Will's jaw tightens. "That a Facebook message?"

"Yep."

"I've been meaning to ask," he says, an edge to his voice that wasn't there before. "Your Facebook bio says to ask about your relationship status." He stops. "Well, I'm asking."

I'm glad it's dark so he can't see my cheeks. I know they're at least three shades of red.

"You know we're in a relationship, William. I just fail to see why my business needs to be broadcast to the world. As long as we know what we are, we're good."

"That's just it," he says. "I'm not sure I know what we are." He pushes past me and heads toward the street.

"William, wait," I say, but he's already halfway to the car. I hate making him feel this way.

In a couple minutes we're parked in my driveway. I hear the music coming from the living room as soon as William walks me to the door. *Exactly what I need at the moment. Awesome…*

"You're an only child, right?" he says.

I nod, my face flaming once again from pink to red to furious.

"Damn, your mom's rocking out in there or something."

"Or something," I mumble. Then to him, "I better see what's going on."

"You need me to come inside with you?"

"No, it's fine. I'll see you tomorrow." A kiss full on the mouth distracts him then I ease him back down the driveway before stepping inside my house. "We're good, right?" I add.

"We are," he replies.

I let out a breath. "I'm so glad. Bye, William," I yell over a cymbal crash. "Mom!" I yell as I shut the door. "What're you doing?"

But I know what she's doing. The same thing she always does when she's alone and drunk. Blaring 80s music through her old stereo, crying, scouring through a gazillion pictures of Dad and Paige. She lied to me. Again.

When I don't find her in the kitchen or living room, I turn the music down and head to her bedroom. She's sitting cross-legged in the middle of her bed, photos of our dead family circling her like hungry sharks. The last hints of her mascara are now faint gray lines on her cheeks, and I can tell by the smell and her matted hair that she's vomited a few times already. She must've opened the vodka right after I left.

"You said you wouldn't drink while I was out."

She ignores the comment like I'm talking to the wall. "Look at this picture of Paige. I think she was six…no, five. Wasn't she cute? Oh, such sweet memories."

I scan the room for liquor bottles, but the only one that's not empty is perched between her legs. I snatch it away.

"Hey, I was drinking that," she says.

"No, you're done."

"You don't tell me what to do—"

"Mom, don't! Just don't." I feel the words in my chest, bubbling over like hot lava from an angry volcano: raging, urgent. I can't stop them, not this time. So I don't. "What does this do for you, Mom, huh?" I hold up the half-empty bottle. "Is it the taste you can't get enough of? Or the making yourself look like a fool? Oh, wait, I know." I touch her stuck-together puke hair. "It's the vomiting, right? That has to be the best part."

"Hey, you can't talk to me like that—"

"Or what?" I ask. "What will you do, huh?" I scoop some photos in my arms then allow them to fall back to the bed. "These people can't be here for you anymore, Mom! This is all you have left of them. They're gone, and they're not coming back! I'm the one who's here, and I bet you couldn't find pictures of me if you wanted to. Where are *my* childhood memories, huh? This has to stop! I'm the one who's here. I'm the one who needs you. I love you, and if you keep drinking…" I hold up a picture of Dad and Paige. "You'll end up dead, just like them. And then I'll have no one."

Mom's glassy eyes search mine. I stare hard into the face that's a much older version of me.

"You could've had something else by now, you know?" I say.

She lowers her head, as if the bed she's perched on is the most interesting thing she's seen all day.

"It's been seventeen years, Mom. You could've met a nice man, had another kid. We could've had so much better than this. Life still goes on around you. You're the only one who's stuck."

"I know," she squeaks out.

Thank God she heard me this time. Needing a tender moment, I sit beside her on the bed and tuck a loose strand of ashen hair behind her ear. "You hungry?"

"Starving."

"I'll make you something." I kiss her forehead and stand up to leave.

"Anna, wait." Mom reaches into her nightstand and pulls out a photo then hands it to me.

My own tears streak my face. "How old was I?"

"I'm not sure. Flip it over."

I turn the picture. "Anna Lucia Berkeley, age four."

She still seems too ashamed to look at me, but mutters through clenched teeth, "Make no mistake, sweet girl. I know where your memories are."

My throat's tight from the tears, but I manage, "We'll be all right, Mom."

"And I'll do better," she adds. "I just need more help."

I nod, silence replacing my words, and head to the kitchen to make her some food.

CHAPTER 3

A biting cold nips my fingers as I step back inside the cabin. Robert's been working in the barn for several hours. He normally signals when I step on the porch, but he must be scrambling to finish before the snow starts falling harder. He's making a second wardrobe for Mr. Besson's store. His supper's no longer warm, but I know him—he'll eat it without complaint. He must be famished by now. Robert Jr.'s been sleeping for at least an hour, and after I feed sweet Emily, she'll find rest as well. I wipe the dishes and set them away, then add another log to the fire before settling in the rocking chair with our infant daughter.

"There's my sweet girl," I say as I nestle our few-weeks-old baby close, readying myself to nurse her. "You are a patient little one. Your brother would have been screaming by now."

Her dark eyes light with anticipation when I position her to me. "You are every bit the spit of your father, do you know that? Do you know how much you look like your pa, precious babe?" I finger her tiny, blond curls and graze her olive-toned cheek with my knuckle. I retrieve a silver rattle that belonged to Robert Jr. and gently shake the toy in her line of vision. "You like that, sweet baby?"

I lean back in the chair, enjoying her warmth and resting my tired body. After several minutes, I hear Robert's boots on the porch. He steps inside quickly when he sees me and our babe rocking in front of the fireplace. He removes his hat, shaking water and snow from the brim, and takes off his coat. He's clutching something beneath it but sets it all beside the door when he notices my glances.

"It's really starting to come down out there," he says. "I've worked up a mean hunger."

"Did you finish the wardrobe?" I whisper, very aware that our infant is nearly asleep.

"I did indeed," he replies softly. "And after we tuck Emily in, I have something else to show you."

"What is it?" Excitement raises my voice a little, causing the baby to whimper.

Robert smiles and puts a finger to his lips. "Shh. I'll show you when the babe's down for the night."

He sets himself on a makeshift stool in front of the fireplace, near us, blowing warm breaths into his clasped hands.

"Your meal," I whisper, pointing to a plate on the nearby table.

"Thank you, my love." He lifts the plate and fork without standing. He remains seated in front of the warmth of the fire and starts eating.

"I'm sorry your supper's cold," I say. "Just let me put the baby down and I'll warm it up for you." I can't help but stare at his coat by the door. I'm sure he's hiding his surprise in it.

"It's fine," he says, dipping a piece of meal bread in duck fat gravy and plunking it in his mouth. "It'll be gone before you have time to warm it. But you are indeed your mother's daughter, sweet Anna: generous, sensitive…and keenly curious." He winks and takes another bite of bread.

"Is that a fact, sir?" I say. "And I feel I should tell you that I find you to be your mother's son as well: arrogant, confident, and insensitive to the words you use with your sweet wife."

He grins as I lift our sleeping baby to my shoulder and button the front of my dress. I rub her back until she's comfortable and Robert joins me when I stand. He follows me to the children's room and stops in front of our son's bed, pulling the quilt up a little higher on our active toddler, who always manages to kick his covers down. I place the baby in her cradle as Robert wraps his arms around me and then leads me to our own bed.

"Now you're all mine," he whispers near my skin, causing my arms to prickle with gooseflesh when his breath tickles my ear. "All mine."

The strength of his arms around me coaxes my body to full awareness. I inhale his scent as he pulls me into his chest—a mixture of sweat, leather, and smoke. I am forever stunned by the way our bodies mold together, like nothing in this icy wilderness could ever feel this warm, this perfect, this well-matched. I belong to him, and he to me.

His kisses trail across my cheek and down my neck. I lift my chin when the stubble of his days-old beard scratches the tender flesh he's now consuming. He reaches for the first button of my dress and I close my eyes, anticipating the feel of his fingers on my willing skin when he whispers, "First, come with me, my love. I have something to show you."

He leads me back into the front of the cabin and lifts his coat from the object it's been disguising. Robert places the item in my hands and my breath catches. It's a wooden box with an ornate flower carved into the top...and the most beautiful gift I've ever received.

"You made this?"

"Most certainly."

"For me?"

"Absolutely."

I can't stop the tears now stinging my chapped, winter

cheeks. "But you could sell this to Mr. Besson—"

Robert is resolute. "It's not for sale, Anna. It's for you." He lifts the lid and pushes a small, shiny latch to one side. A dainty, angelic melody floats into the air.

"Oh my! It's a music box." I raise it closer to my ears. "I've never owned a music box before." I search Robert's face. "How did you do this?"

He smiles as if his whole world is invested in this one moment. "Well, Mr. Besson sells the music-makers. He says they come all the way from France. I made an extra butter churn on trade for it."

"France," I repeat, running my fingers along the grooves in the lid.

"I was a little concerned at first that I wouldn't be able to mount the music-maker inside the box properly, but I think it works mighty fine. Do you like it, my darling?"

I'm only able to manage four words. "I love you, Robert."

I'm reminded of how big and strong his hands are when they lift me off the floor and into his arms. These hands, always busy and in motion: chopping firewood, crafting furniture, playing his fiddle, tossing our son into the air until he squeals with delight. The only time they're still is when he's holding our baby girl, says grace over our meals, or when he's holding me.

Robert drops our bodies on the bed when we reach our room. He covers my tiny frame like a shadow from a great tree on a sapling. We meld together: lips, tongues, skin.

"You are my weakness, Anna," he whispers near the lobe of my ear, sending shivers down my neck and arms. "Only you. Always you…"

He looks in my eyes, his mouth curved up into that smile again that seems to come from the most hidden part of his soul.

"Will you kiss me again?" I ask.

"You never have to ask to be kissed, my love," he whispers. "Not ever." He kisses me over and over and I knit my fingers into his blond curls, forcing his kisses to deepen, needing to be close, immediate, urgently near him until he's no longer himself but part of me.

The first time I made love to Robert on our wedding night, I felt something I'd never experienced before: hope, inspiration, a future outside of the harsh realities that are life in the newly sprung Michigan Territories. Every young woman dreams of marriage, children, and a home of her own. But I never imagined this. Robert is beyond any bit of magic I ever dreamed of.

He nibbles my upper lip, then teases the bottom one as well. I close my eyes, savoring the feel of his hand on my stomach and his lips on mine. "Robert," I say, breaking the kiss to look in his eyes, "if this is a dream, I never want to awaken."

"You won't, my love," he replies. "You won't…"

But I do, every time my alarm goes off. I slide a finger across my phone's screen to silence it and then run my hands over my arms to tame the goose bumps. I can still feel his touch on my skin and his lips on my mouth. I sink deeper into the covers and close my eyes so tightly I see stars. I want to be with Robert a little longer. I'm not ready to leave, never want to let him go. But now my face is too wet with tears to sleep. Robert's gone, trapped in our wilderness memories until I'm lucky enough to dream again. And I'm here without him. Always here…

I swipe the tears until the remnants of eyeliner I failed to remove last night are simply black smudges on my face. *She* stares back at me from the mirror—the Anna of the wild, the Anna who misses her husband and babies, the Anna who's as broken as her mother, no matter how hard she tries to pretend she's okay. *Me…*

How can I accuse Mom of living in the past and never letting go when I'm holding on to a past from a couple hundred years ago? I know what I have to do. I pick up my phone again and open Facebook. No one will ever need to ask about my relationship status again. I type his name and read my new status update: *Anna Berkeley is in a relationship with William Hull.*

***

"You feeling okay?" I ask Mom when I'm in the kitchen.

"I'll be all right," she says, her glassy eyes betraying the confidence in her words. "But I guess I only have me to blame, huh?" She tugs on her name badge until *Vikki Berkeley* is even with the pocket on her blouse. I'm not sure why she's so concerned about the symmetry of her badge, anyway—nothing else about Mom is balanced this morning. Typical Monday.

She meets me at the table and presses a hand on top of mine. She's always had such gorgeous hands, long fingers and manicured nails. But now I see a gazillion tiny wrinkles. Her skin looks thin, worn out. She has a few gray hairs now too, but I'm pretending I haven't noticed those. I pretend not to notice a lot of things lately.

"How about you?" Mom asks. "You okay?"

"Sure," I reply. "Why do you ask?"

"Well, it sounded like you were dreaming last night. You were moaning."

Oh God. "Huh, that's weird. Maybe I was. I don't remember." I hate lying to her, but I'd hate telling her the truth even more, when it comes to my past-life memories.

"I'm sorry about the last couple of days," she says. "I'll try to do better."

"I know," I say. It's what I always say. "Well, I better go. I need to beat the school buses or I'll be stuck in traffic forever. Have a good day at work."

"I love you, Anna."

"I know. I love you too, Mom."

In a few seconds, I'm out the door and sitting in my

car. "Come on, come on. Start already." The car finally spits and sputters to life on the fourth crank and I let out a breath. "That a girl, Blue Wombat."

My friend Maggie is the one who nicknamed my old-as-dirt Dodge Neon the Blue Wombat because the first time I picked her up in it, so much mud was caked under the front bumper that it looked like the car had been burrowing. Truth be known, that girl is just a complete animal freak and watches way too much Animal Planet. But, I like Blue Wombat. It seems to fit it somehow. I just hope it keeps running until I can save up enough money to have a tune-up. I'm a little afraid to know what's really going on under her hood.

In a few minutes I'm in my designated parking spot, locking the Wombat's doors. It's crazy just how suffocating the heat really is. I slide my sunglasses to the top of my head, swearing the *yes-I'm-back-with-a-vengeance* humidity is solely responsible for keeping them there instead of my *a-little-too-poofy-today* hair. I scan the sizzling parking lot for Maggie. I hear her before I see her.

"Girl, I saw that you finally changed your relationship status on Facebook. I bet William juices his pants when he sees it."

"Yuck! Crude, Mags." But I laugh.

Maggie hitches her book bag higher on her bony shoulder. "I know, but you have to admit, he's way intense."

"I know, but he's sweet. And I really like him a lot."

"Obviously," she says. "Now hurry up before the damn tardy bell rings." As she pulls me behind her into the crowded hallway, Maggie chants, "Excuse me. Pardon me. Girl in a relationship coming through."

"You are a certifiable nut," I say when she pushes me ahead of her and slaps me on the butt.

"Yeah, well, it's been a whole year since I've been in a relationship, so let me live vicariously through you for a little while, okay?"

"You could have any guy in this school," I remind her, "so don't act all pitiful."

"I know," she says, "but still…" She winks and I crack up.

And she *could* have any guy in this school. Maggie is everyone's standard of beauty: blond hair, blue eyes, and a tiny little body that looks like she works out constantly, but the girl can devour a whole bag of Doritos without blinking. But what attracts me to her is her sense of humor and drive. She hasn't seriously dated anyone in a year because she doesn't want to be attached-at-the-hip to someone and then leave for college next fall. Like I said, *drive*. But I also happen to know that she likes dating tons of different guys with no strings attached. Yeah, she doesn't fool me one bit.

We make it to homeroom before the tardy bell rings and I pull out my Calculus homework to look it over before first block starts. I know I have a few wrong answers, but at least I try. Dustin Mears looks at Maggie when he passes her desk and blurts out, "What up, Maggie the Jaggie?"

"Stop calling me that!" She swats his ass with a notebook. "It stopped being funny like two years ago."

"No it didn't." He laughs.

We're the Northridge Jaguars, and our male mascot is Mick Jaguar and our female one is Maggie the Jaggie. I've always thought it would be hilarious for Maggie to try out for mascot because of that fact, but Maggie, not so much.

"Anna, we have to switch schools like right now," she says when Dustin starts kissing her on the cheek to make up for his transgression.

"*We*?" I say. "Why *we*?"

"Because you're my person," Maggie says as she pushes him playfully away and he sits down in the desk behind her. "Where I go, you go."

I shake my head. "Yeah, yeah. Just suck it up, diva." I receive a text and look at my phone. It's William.

I saw the new fb status. Nice <3 meet me
at the mall after football practice.

I'm still smiling when our teacher stands up to start class.

***

It'll probably be another hour before William gets here. His practices usually last 'til five. I text Mom to tell her I won't be home when she gets there, then I stand in line at Cinnabon, my guilty pleasure. I find a bench to sit and people-watch—my favorite thing to do in the mall—while I tear an edge from my cinnamon roll and pop it in my mouth.

I'm not sure why I'm so nervous about seeing Will in a little while. I know committing to our relationship is the right thing to do. After all, I'd never want him to think I'm just stringing him along, and I *do* like him. But no matter how hard I try to push it to the back of my mind, I'm still remembering my dream about Robert. His hands are what I can't shake from my overactive brain. Everything about his hands coaxes my body to full awareness. Those strong, capable hands are what made our living and protected us from danger. Those hands helped me bring our babies into the world and tuck them in on bitter winter nights. Those hands grasped the sides of my face and positioned me where he wanted my mouth for anticipated lines of kisses, or tangled in my hair and tugged just a little, letting me know his urgency and desire. He knew just how to touch me, hold me, utterly melt me into him until I was no longer myself but one with him. Sometimes when I think about those hands, I forget everything else in the world. I forget everything else in the world but Robert.

Remembering that William will be here in a little while, I curse myself for the millionth time for daydreaming of what will never be again, and stand up to toss my Cinnabon wrapper in the nearby trash bin. I sit on the bench again and scoot over a little when I feel someone sit down next to me.

"Excuse me, but do you mind if I sit here?"

My stomach clenches and I lose my breath. Every nerve in my body stands on end, but I can't move. I'm totally frozen in terror. Even without looking at him, I know that voice! But, it can't be. I close my eyes before turning my head to confirm my wild suspicions.

When my gaze meets his, I know the only thing I've ever known for my entire life.

It's Robert.

CHAPTER 4

"I…" But it's all I can manage. I'm paralyzed, staring at the face that has flooded my dreams for five years, and I'm so overwhelmed with fear and emotion that I can't move. How is he here? This can't be real.

"Are you okay?" Robert says. Robert—*my* nineteenth century Robert—sitting right here next to me in a pair of khaki walking shorts and a white polo shirt, wants to know if I'm okay. "I can leave if you want me to," he adds. His eyes search my face and I can tell he's holding back, like any hint of approval on my part would allow him to take me into his arms without hesitation and never let me go.

"N-no," I say. "Don't leave. But…how?"

"How what?" He gets a weird look. "Ma'am, do you need help with something?"

Is it possible he doesn't know who I am? Is my mind playing some kind of vicious joke on me? I swallow hard and force myself to say the words. "How are you here…*Robert*?"

He lets out a breath like he's been holding it from the moment he sat down. "Oh, my Anna. My God! You know me."

I bolt, every force in my body pulling, tugging, coaxing

me to run. How is this happening? It can't be real. I move quickly through a crowd of people, tears flooding my cheeks before I realize it. I can hear Robert a short distance behind me, saying my name, causing my chest to tighten so much I can barely breathe. I'm not sure why I'm running away from the only thing I've ever hungered for. Probably because, until this point, he's been nothing more than a dream, a pain so deep and lost in the past that the only safety I had in his love was knowing that it had *once* existed, had *once* been real and true. You're not supposed to touch a dream when you're wide awake. My head's spinning so much I fear I may faint, so I sit on the next empty bench I see. I take a few deep breaths just to appease my aching lungs, and I lock eyes with Robert when he's in front of me again.

"I'm so sorry I scared you, Anna." He's smiling so wide I'm afraid his face might break. "It's just that…you've never recognized me before."

"Before?" My head is reeling. What does he mean *before*?

"You'll never know how much I've missed you," he says.

"But—I don't understand."

Robert looks at me with a tenderness I haven't seen in this lifetime. "Please, may I sit? We need to talk." I nod and he obliges. "I didn't expect your reaction when you saw me, Anna. Like I said, this is new. You've never recognized me before."

"Why do you keep saying that? I've never recognized you before?"

"Because we've—" But then he stops. "You know, I think it might be better if you tell me what *you* remember."

Tell him what I remember? Do I tell him that I remember his hands on my body and his lips on mine? Or do I tell him that I remember loving him, being his wife and the mother of his children? Or maybe I should tell him that I remember brutal winters and times of hunger when the only warmth and nourishment ever afforded to us was each other. When it comes to Robert Grafton, I only truly remember one fact: that he was my everything.

"I've been having dreams for the past five years—dreams of us in another life in the wilderness. I know it was in the 1800s. We were married and had two children—a boy and a girl." I look in the rich, brown eyes so familiar from my dreams. "I'm actually wondering if I'm sleeping right now." He smiles, and my chest feels like it might explode. "Anyway, that's what I remember."

Robert looks entranced, completely mesmerized by my words. I know I'm staring, but I can't help it. He's the same: blond curls, broad shoulders, and a hint of a beard that makes me wonder if he's unshaven for my benefit. When I allow myself to look at his hands, my mind shifts to me in his arms, his large palm on the small of my back, his fingers firmly pressing me into him. When I realize where my thoughts have drifted, I stare at the floor instead.

"So, you only remember our *last* lifetime together…" he mutters.

The words jar me, punch me, hit me like bricks to the face. "Our *last* lifetime together?" I have to catch my breath. "You mean…there have been more?"

His single word derails me. "Yes."

Everything's spinning again and I close my eyes, attempting to ease my shaky nerves. After a few deep breaths, I look at Robert again, needing for something, for anything at all to make sense. "So tell me," I say to the beautiful ghost beside me. "What do *you* remember?"

He says a single word again. "Everything." When I'm quiet, he continues. "You know, this is usually the toughest part for me. I'm always the stranger, finding a way to approach the sweetest, most beautiful girl I've ever known. The girl who has forever been my whole world, and yet she doesn't know me. Winning your affections over and over can be…challenging."

I ask the first thing that comes to mind. "So, how did you find me?"

He's resolute. "Well, somehow, I always find you."

The words ripple waves of chills down my arms, and I rub them for relief.

"I will say, though," he continues, "finding you this time was a breeze compared to the others. Thank God for the Digital Age. I found you on Facebook about three years ago, so I started saving up so I could go to college here. I had to take a year off after I graduated from high school in South Carolina just to save enough to enroll at the University of Alabama. But I managed to do it, and here I am." He takes another deep breath. "And there you are."

He's rambling, obviously waiting for me to say something. But all I can think about is the fact that he'd made plans for me, centered his whole life around finding me. And we've had *more* lifetimes together. I'm still trying to make sense of what's happening. "So," I say, "you're a freshman at Alabama? But you took a year off—"

"I'm nineteen," he says before I can ask his age. "And I know you're seventeen. There's always a two-year difference in our ages."

As badly as I want to know how Robert's here—how we're *both* here in this lifetime—I feel like I can't breathe. I need some fresh air, now. "This is too much for me," I say. "I need some time to think."

Robert exhales. "Oh God, Anna, please know that if I would've had any idea that you'd recognize me, I would've never just walked up to you like that."

"What *would* you have done then?" I ask.

"You know what? I'm not sure. Believe me, from the moment I found you on Facebook, I wanted to hitchhike to Alabama just to be with you, but I knew I couldn't do that. I had to do this the right way, be self-sufficient, have something to offer you. I don't know…"

We exchange awkward laughs, then he pulls a small

card from his shirt pocket. "Here. It has my number and address on it. I live in an apartment on campus. Call me after you've had some time to think, okay? We have a lot to talk about."

The tips of our fingers touch when he hands me the card, and it's like every sensation I've ever felt in my body awakens at once. He holds my stare, obviously gauging my reaction to him. All I can think about are his eyes piercing through mine, and the desire I so clearly see in them. If we were our former selves, this would be the moment right before our lips touch. Then he would take me into his arms. But instead, I drop my hand quickly and pretend that the sparks created between us aren't real, even though nothing has ever been more real in my life.

"I'll call you soon," I say.

"I'll be counting the minutes," he replies. "Bye, Anna."

I tuck the card in my jeans pocket and walk away. When I'm out of the mall and almost to my car, the tears start and don't stop. Waves of the young woman I was two hundred years ago crash onto the shore of the girl I am now. Everything I thought I would never be again—*could* never be again—now crushes me in confusion. How is Robert here? Still alive? Reborn? How am *I* here? Where are the children our love created? Are they dead? In Heaven? Are they reborn, too? Does everyone just recycle, or are we the only ones? We have to be. I know this isn't normal. I have so many questions, and Robert is the only one who can answer them. And as terrified as I am of this new reality, I know that when I calm down, I have to reach out to him.

I unlock the Wombat's doors and slide into the driver's seat. I look at the mall entrance again, and a sigh escapes my lips. *My Robert is in that building.* I'm pulled from my thoughts when my phone sounds a text alert. I glance at the screen. Oh God! I forgot about William. I open his message.

I'm here. Where are you?

I push through the pangs of guilt and type:

Had to leave. Not feeling well.

Not exactly a lie, but nowhere near the truth, either. I've never felt more alive in this lifetime. I quickly pull into traffic and head toward the only person who'll understand.

***

"Rose? Are you awake?" I know she is, but I always feel like I need to ask before entering her room, even when the door's open.

"Anna, darling, what a pleasant surprise. Come in, come in." She points the remote toward her television. "Let me turn this thing off. It's only noise and bother anyway." She grimaces when she looks me full in the face. "Is everything all right, dear?"

"Yeah, fine." I sit in front of the large picture window in Rose's room. It's her favorite spot. Usually on my Saturday morning rounds, we sit and drink our coffee and watch the cars pull in and out of the parking spots in front. We like identifying which visitors belong to which residents. Sometimes I find it depressing, but I'd never say that to Rose. She enjoys it too much.

"Well, we can't drink coffee this late in the day," Rose says when she joins me.

"I know, and there's not nearly as many cars today."

"Saturdays are the prime visiting days, my dear. You picked a bad time to people-watch." She places a thin, wrinkled hand on top of mine. "Now tell me, what's wrong?"

The tears come again, and I look into Rose's shiny teal eyes. "I saw him."

"Saw who, dear?"

"Robert."

"You had another dream?" The corners of her mouth droop. "Oh, did something bad happen? Tell me all about it."

"No." I face her and cover her hand with my free one. "You don't understand. Rose, I just saw Robert in the mall. He's alive and well, just like me. Rose…Robert is here."

She's quiet, absorbing my words. I'm waiting for her to panic, gasp for air, say there's no way it was Robert and that I'm a raving lunatic, but she doesn't do any of that. Instead, a smile stretches across her lips like she's just seen the ocean for the first time.

"Oh, Anna, that's wonderful! Now you know why you're having those dreams, huh? It's a miracle."

"A miracle?" I'm confused. "Yeah, I guess, but I'm terrified. I mean, how can he be here? Why is this happening? I'm not sure what to do—"

"Shhh." She stands. "Come here."

I lean into her hug and rest in the silence for a moment, breathing in her scent of coconut body lotion and vapor rub.

"Now," she says, "let me tell you what I know about fear. It's the one thing that will keep you from ever experiencing the best things in life. Going to college, getting a job, falling in love, getting married, having babies—all scary things. But, they're also some of the best things that will ever happen to you, things most people hope for all their lives. You've got the chance to have them in more than one life. You can't let something like a little fear stop you from living, Anna. And I mean *really* living."

I know what Rose is trying to do, but this is different. This isn't *a little fear*. This is a level of scary that's beyond the scope of normal. Mere minutes ago I was standing face to face with the man I've been in love with throughout time. My soulmate. And I'm frightened, renewed, and grateful all at once. My skin tingles, every emotion I've ever felt coursing through my body like a flood. She's right, Robert and I are a miracle. I don't doubt that for a second. But that still doesn't explain why. Why is this happening?

"So, did you get a chance to talk to him?" Rose asks.

"Yes, and he said we've lived other lifetimes together, not just the one in the wilderness."

Rose murmurs, "Amazing."

"And he remembers all of them, but apparently this is the first time I've ever remembered anything about us. He didn't expect me to know him when he walked up to me."

"Oh, child, I guess you nearly fainted when you saw him! What did you do?"

My cheeks pinken. "I ran."

We both laugh and it feels good—better than I've felt in a long time, actually. Talking to Rose always grounds me, even when I'm so far from Earth, balloons should envy me.

"Well, promise me you won't keep running from him. Okay, child?" I nod and she cups my chin like I'm twelve. "I mean it, Anna. I'm going to tell you something, and I want you to listen. Let's sit." When we're seated again, she says, "All my life, I was so full of talent, had so much to offer the world, and I took it all for granted until I lost Teddy and then Ted, and I ended up in here. Do you know I used to give free piano lessons to less fortunate children?"

"You told me that," I say.

"I'm sure I did," she says, "but have I ever told you just how *well* I played piano?"

"Oh, I just assumed—"

"You assumed, but when I was your age, piano was my life. I had aspirations to attend the conservatory, but I met Ted and well, the rest is history. Even though I don't regret for one moment marrying my sweetheart, part of me always wished I had furthered my music beyond just playing in a small symphony and at weddings and funerals. And as gratifying as it was to teach those children, I always wondered if I could have done more. But then I wound up here." She looks around the small room. "Now my regrets are different."

I'm hooked on her words. "What do you mean?"

"I mean that when I could still play, it didn't really matter where or for whom. I was valuable, contributed to those around me. Do you know what I am in here? I'm small, ant-sized. I contribute nothing."

"That's not true," I say, her words stinging like salt on parched lips. "You're so important to me, Rose. You should know that."

"I do, sweet girl," she replies, "and that's why I never want you to have any regrets. All that time I wasted, wondering if I could have been more, fearing that I would always feel like a failure for not doing bigger things with my music, I should have spent that time enjoying my talent and the contributions I was making then. I never want you to have regrets, Anna. And if you don't go to Robert and explore this gift the universe has given you, then you'll regret it for the rest of your life. And maybe in the next one, too."

I'm out of my chair again and plopped on the floor in front of her. I wrap my arms around her legs and lay my head on her lap. "Thank you, Rose. I do know that I love Robert, it's just that somewhere in the back of my mind, I still didn't believe it was all real. Now that I know it is, it's overwhelming."

"You'll be fine, honey. I promise."

"I love you, Rose."

"I love you too, sweet girl."

When I allow myself to remember the last dream I had of me and Robert, my heart beats fast but fragile, like a bird's. I feel the quickened beats against Rose's knees and wonder if she notices. "Why do you think Robert and I keep coming back? Do you think we did something wrong?"

Rose cups my face and smiles. "No, child. I think you keep coming back to show this wretched world what true love is all about."

I smile at her reasoning, and we sit in the quiet until darkness blankets the room.

***

I sniff the coffee's steam, and not the regular kind, but the hazelnut kind that Mom likes. I like it too, I guess, but plain old coffee is still my favorite—plain coffee with lots of sugar and cream. But the hazelnut is all we have. Maybe it was too late for Rose to drink coffee this evening, but not me. It never keeps me awake. Besides, something else totally different will be keeping me up tonight. So far I've focused on the coffee, my bedroom, my homework that's still unfinished, anything but the fact that I met a flesh-and-bone Robert today…until now. I look at the card he gave me, so tempted to call him that I almost do, but I simply put his number in my phone instead. I turn the card over and over in my hand. This is Robert's handwriting, the first real object I have in this lifetime that we've both touched. I place the card to my lips and inhale. *Robert…*

He said he found me on Facebook a few years back, then it hits me. *Oh God!* I updated my relationship status. Today. I wonder if Robert's seen it too? Is that why he went ahead and sought me out now, before my relationship with William gets more serious? My relationship with William…now my stomach hurts and I nudge the coffee far enough away that I can't smell it. Why couldn't Robert have shown up a few months ago, instead? Is the universe playing some kind of sick joke on me? You know, besides the joke where Robert and I keep coming back? Every snag I've ever had with William stems from the fact that I remembered my past life. And now Robert's here.

So William and I are over.

But I still want to break it off with Will as painlessly as possible—if that's even a possibility at all. He's going to be hurt, I know it. And why couldn't I have waited just one more stupid day to update my relationship status? Yeah, the universe is a twisted sister.

I cross over to the desk and open my laptop. Robert's obviously been watching my Facebook account closely. I'm sure that means he must have one, too. I click into the Facebook search bar and hesitate before typing his name. Rose has probably asked me a dozen times by now if I had any plans to research my past with Robert. No part of me has ever had any desire to try and make sense of us. Robert, our babies, our past life together—those have been the real and true things in my life, the constant that's pure and unblemished instead of grief-lined and broken. And I'll be damned if I've ever wanted to soil that escape in any way. But now he's here, and it's difficult—will never be simple again. I take a deep breath and type the words: *Robert Grafton.*

He's the third Robert from the top, and I sigh when his smiling profile picture enters my line of vision. Giddiness courses through my veins as freely as blood as I stare at his image, burning it deeper into my already scorching brain. Robert is as perfect in this lifetime as the last: his sincere, full-of-life eyes, strong shoulders, thick sun-kissed curls, and impeccable jawline. I'd bet a million girls have thrown themselves at him in the last couple of years—maybe the past hundred years. No way in hell he'd step into my school without chicks falling all over him like lovesick middle-schoolers.

I click to my own profile and stare at the words: *In a relationship with William Hull.* I want to change it back to *Single,* hoping more than anything that Robert hasn't noticed it, will let me explain that William and I really aren't that serious. But I know I can't change it back, not until I talk to William. He deserves a clean break-up. I'd never want him to think I was playing games. And I know I shouldn't feel weird about my FB status anyway. After all, I never knew Robert was here—couldn't possibly know something that mind-blowing. But I feel guilty anyway, feel guilty that I introduced myself to William at that concert, guilty that I have to hurt him, guilty that I took off today when I saw Robert. Then, another thought enters my spinning brain. I click back to Robert's profile and look at his relationship status. Two words assault me:

It's complicated.

Is he seeing someone, too? Just stringing her along in case he didn't find me? My stomach is playing host to a butterfly tennis match, but I click on the box containing Robert's photos anyway. I have to know who this other girl is. I start scrolling through his images and lose my breath. *Oh God...*

Dozens of sketches fill the screen as I stare. There's one of me standing on the porch of our cabin, and one of me on the day we were married. Another of me on a wild horse that took me two weeks to break. She was the first gift Robert ever gave me, in the wilderness times. I named her Spirit. Then there are ones I don't recognize. The clothing looks almost medieval. I'm beyond fascinated. Those have to be me in the lifetimes I don't remember. But Robert remembers...he remembers *everything*. I allow the tears to soak my cheeks as I take in each image. Robert mastered my face right down to the last detail, even the yellow flecks that touch my green eyes. He knows every inch of me. Complicated doesn't even begin to describe it. I retrieve my phone and touch Robert's name.

Even my Spirit couldn't keep me away.

CHAPTER 5

I told Mom it would be impossible to finish my homework without a visit to the university library. Homework is the one lie that effectively gets me out of the house on a school night. But the campus apartments are different from the library, so I'm a little unsure of where I'm going, exactly. Some of the girls at school brag about hanging with college guys. They probably know this area as well as they know the route to Starbucks or McDonalds, but not me. I grip the Wombat's steering wheel tighter and scan the numbers on the student apartments, when I'm finally in front of them. Robert's has to be in the general vicinity. When I locate his door, I find a decent parking spot and pull in. But I don't get out of the car right away. I'm very aware that from the moment I'm with him again, in the here and now, life as I have known it will cease to be. And it's scary, but that's all you can really expect from the unknown, anyway.

When I'm out of the car, I tuck my keys and phone into the front pocket of my jean shorts and smooth the front of my favorite ruffled tank top. I run my fingers through my hair and check my reflection in the car window. I take a deep breath to stave off my shaky nerves, and make my way to his door. When I knock, I hear some shuffling around inside his apartment. My heart's beating out of my chest.

"Hey, Anna," Robert says as he opens the door. "I'm so glad you called me. Come in."

A flood of adrenaline rushes through me, and I notice several things at once—his broad chest and right-from-the-shower scent, his still damp hair and the hint of awkwardness in his voice. He's like a friendly stranger to me, and yet I know him better than any guy I've ever met. In the wilderness, Robert and I were often alone. And we spoke of nothing and everything in the same conversation most days. But now I'm not sure *how* to talk to him. I wonder if he feels the same dread—the dread of wanting that kinship back but not sure if it can ever be the same again. I follow him inside, hoping the sudden flush of heat washing over my face isn't noticeable.

"Did you find the place okay?" he asks.

"It wasn't bad," I reply, realizing that I'm staring but unable to stop. I'm too aware that he's my flesh-and-bone dream come true.

"Are you thirsty? I have some sodas in the fridge."

"I'm good." I notice him glancing at my legs. He diverts his gaze when he knows he's busted.

He throws a boyish grin in my direction. "I'm sorry. It's just that your clothing was always a lot more modest in the past. I will admit, though, I really like the freedom of this era." He points to his own shorts. "Don't get me wrong—I'm including my clothing options, too. And washing machines are pretty awesome, am I right?"

I let out a nervous laugh, loosening the tension in my chest a bit. Thank God Robert still has his sense of humor and ease of speech. We sit on the couch and I'm quiet at first, taking in the lines of his face and the shine in his eyes. He's scanning every inch of my face as well, but I don't mind. I totally understand his need to simply be with me, to look at me.

"So, tell me about yourself." Robert winks, a twitch of awkwardness turning up the corners of his mouth.

"Ha, I bet you've used that line on dozens of girls, huh?"

He smiles but doesn't acknowledge the comment. "I guess we have a lot to talk about," he says instead. "So, first things first. Tell me about your life here in Alabama, Anna."

Where do I start? Do I dare tell him that I have so much responsibility at home that even the weight of my clothes drags me down most days? Or that unlike most teens, I dread weekends because Mom will be drinking again? Or maybe I should... No, this is Robert. I lower the shield and just let go. "There's not really a lot to tell. I was born here in Tuscaloosa. It's just me and my mom. My dad and eight-year-old sister were killed in a car accident while Mom was pregnant for me, so I never knew them—"

"Oh, that's horrible. I'm so sorry." A pained expression consumes him.

"Yeah, me too, and my mom has a drinking problem. She's been in rehab a few times. It helps, and she'll be good for a while, but it never sticks. Actually, she needs rehab again now. I have to help her out a lot. I'm all she has." He's caught up in my words, so I just keep going. "Let's see, I'm a senior at Northridge, and I volunteer at the convalescent home on weekends. They call us Sunshine Warriors. I'm trying to earn the merit scholarship the organization gives each year so I'll have some extra money for college. I really like the old people I interact with, too. They're great. I guess that's about it."

"Volunteer work with the elderly, huh?" Robert smiles and my legs get all squirmy. I hope the shudders dancing in my belly aren't noticeable. "That doesn't surprise me," he adds. "You've always had such a big heart. It's one of the things I love most about you."

He realizes what he's blurted out, and backpedals, "Oh, you know what I mean, right, Anna? That came out too fast and too soon, but you know what I meant…" He reminds me of a fish on a hook, gasping and wide-eyed.

I throw him a life ring. "It's fine, Robert. I know what you meant. And, thank you. It was a really sweet compliment, actually."

He takes, what I'm guessing, is a much-needed breath. "Oh, good."

I need to lighten the mood. "Okay, so tell me again why you chose the University of Alabama?"

He grins. "I would think that answer would be obvious. *You.*"

Now I'm the fish on the hook. "Oh, I know. I was kidding."

The smile I've missed for two hundred years dances on his lips again. "Well, like I said earlier, I'm from South Carolina. I found you on Facebook in the middle of my junior year of high school. That's when I started saving my own money for college so I could be close to you. I checked your profile often just to make sure you didn't move or anything. After I graduated, I still didn't have enough money saved to move here. So I worked another year, and now I'm finally here."

"You worked and saved money for years…just to be close to me?"

"I would do anything for you, Anna."

I'm so touched I have to hold back tears. "That had to be so hard. Wow."

"Nah, not really. The working and saving money was the easy part. It was the being away from you that was tough. I've wanted to move to Alabama since that first moment I found you."

Our eyes lock as we realize that every moment we've ever shared together always ends up in a love so all-consuming, we'd move time and space to be in it.

"So," Robert says, "about what we remember in our pasts, do you want to start?"

"No, you go. I mean, you're the one who remembers

everything, right?" I swallow and then admit, "I saw your Facebook earlier tonight…the sketches of me. They were amazing. Tell me, Robert, how is this happening?"

He gets a faraway look and I'm hanging on his every movement. I can almost see the air escaping his lips when he says, "This is the fourth time we've been reborn. Our first lifetime was in the 1300s. I was born in 1368 and you in 1370. Like I said, there's always a couple of years between us. We were both born in Canterbury, England, and remained there after we were married.

"Our second lifetime was in the 1500s. I was born in 1562 in London and you were born in 1564 in Stratford-upon-Avon. Your family moved to London when you were fourteen. Thank God, or I might never have found you again, but it wouldn't be from lack of trying. I stared into the face of every damsel I crossed paths with, always looking for you. We stayed in London after we were married. And, well, you remember our third lifetime together, so—"

"No, keep going," I insist. "I only remember what I've seen in my dreams. I can't do what you're doing…recall dates or places, or even our families and friends. Please tell me what you know, Robert. I need to know more about our wilderness times."

He takes my hands in his and I freeze, captured by the heat of his touch and warmth of his words. "I was born in 1786 and you in 1788. We were both born in the Northwest Territory, but lived in what is now known as the Michigan Territory after we were married. We had our two babies—"

"Robert Jr. and Emily," I say.

"That's right." He swallows away the cracking tone of his voice at the mention of our children.

"When were they born?" I ask. "I've always wanted to know their birthdays."

"Robert Jr. was born May 2, 1804 and Emily was born on July 15, 1805."

"My babies," I whisper, fighting back the tears now filling my eyes. "I miss them so much. Maybe they're the reason I..." Then I ask, "Did we have children in our other lifetimes, too?"

Robert's jaw tightens. "No."

My head's spinning, but I focus on what seems like a million questions swirling in my brain. "My name was Anna Lucia Berkeley back then and yours was Robert Thomas Grafton, just like present day. Have we had those same names every time?"

"We have," he replies.

"So, I'm guessing we have the same extended families, then?" My chest tightens when I think about Dad. "Was my dad alive in any of the lifetimes, or did he die before I was born then, too?"

Robert gets a funny look.

"I was just wondering since I never had the chance to meet him here, you know."

"Anna, listen." His voice softens. "We have the same names, but our extended families have been different in every lifetime. We both had mothers and fathers, but they weren't the same people...not ever. I'm sorry."

I search his eyes. "So you've never recognized other people from our past lives?"

Robert clears his throat. "No, Anna. We're the ones who keep repeating. It's just us."

"Wow." It's all I can say. I mean, it's really not a newsflash. I have enough common sense to know that if everyone lived multiple lifetimes, it would seem as normal as breathing. But this is far from normal.

"So, you still haven't told me what *you* remember about us," Robert says. "I thought I was gonna pass out when you said my name in the mall today. I have to admit, though, I'm so relieved that you remember me. It makes it so much easier." He takes my hand and places it between both of his.

My heart speeds to a dangerous rhythm, and I'm fully

aware that this is the first time Robert has held my hand when I'm not asleep. I try in vain to slow my racing heart, to think of anything but him. But instead, I become acutely aware of his fingers, his skin, the slightest movement of his thumb across the top of my hand...of him. My awareness of his every breath is making it impossible to concentrate, so I slide my hand out of his light grasp and stand up. It'll be easier to tell him about my dreams if he's not holding my hand.

"The dreams started about five years ago," I say. "The first dream I had of us was the day we met in the wilderness times. I was down by the river dousing laundry that was too dirty for just the washtub, and you rode up next to me to water your horse. I remember thinking you were the most handsome man I'd ever seen. And that's just it, I could see you, hear you, smell you. I was there...with you. I woke up the next morning terrified and curious all at once. And I knew it wasn't just a dream."

Robert stands and joins me. "How?"

"Because it was five years ago, and I was only twelve when I had my first dream of you. I rationalized that it had to be real. There was no other way I could know those details about the 1800s, about you and me. No way *any* twelve-year-old girl could know those things. It was just too real not to be real, know what I mean?"

"More than you know." Robert bows his head like he's praying. There's a moment of stillness between us.

I clear my throat and continue, "The next dream occurred about four months later. You and I were having a picnic by that same river...and you asked me to be your bride."

He smiles like the memory's food and he's been starving. "I did indeed. You said yes, and for the third time I was the happiest man on Earth." He takes my hand again. "We've had a lot of firsts, Anna. The firsts are always my favorite."

I ignore my flushing cheeks and keep talking, fearing

the words will be lost in his eyes if I stop. "There were more dreams of us, riding horses, taking walks, but when I was sixteen, I dreamed of our wedding night. You carried me over the threshold of our cabin you'd built with your own two hands. I remember feeling so in love with everything about you, like I was the luckiest girl in the world. But this dream wasn't like others I'd ever experienced…"

Robert holds the edge of my words in his stare. My stomach's trembling hard enough to crush butterflies, but I force the sentences out. "When you made love to me for the first time in that dream, I *felt* it—every kiss, every touch, every shiver. If I had ever questioned whether or not you were real, all doubt left me in those moments. You were more real to me than my mom, my friends, my life. After that night, you became my whole world. And all I ever looked forward to after that dream was to fall asleep and have you with me."

Before I manage another breath, I'm in his arms. Robert crushes my face against his chest and knits his hands into my hair. "I've missed you so much, my love. You don't know how long I've waited just to hold you again."

But I do know, so much so that my whole body's shaking. He tenses in response then takes my face in his hands. "You're trembling. Please don't be afraid of me. I'd never hurt you, my sweet Anna…not in a million years."

I'm terrified and embarrassed in the same breath. "I'm not afraid of you, Robert. You just don't get it, do you? Until today in that mall, you were a dream. And in all my dreams, there's only you and me. Then last year I dreamed about Robert Jr. A few months ago, I had my first dream about baby Emily. I even dreamed of you last night. You gave me a gift—a wooden music box. Do you remember it?"

His breath quickens. "Do I remember it? Nothing could ever make me forget."

"Last night you were a dream." I place a hand on his chest, his heartbeat like a distant drum. Memories of moments like this with him surface before I can push them under for the zillionth time. "You were only a dream," I say again, "and now you're here."

It takes every ounce of strength I can muster to tug away from his grasp when he leans in to kiss me. I want him to the point of madness, but I know I can't do this. Not yet. There's still someone else to consider. But I'm not sure how to do this, how to tell him about William.

"Robert, wait."

"I'm sorry. I just thought—"

"Don't apologize," I reply. "It's just that, I'm kind of seeing someone."

He backs away like I'm a fragile thing and he's dynamite. "Seeing someone?"

Oh God. He doesn't know, obviously hasn't seen my new Facebook status. "We've only been dating a couple of months, though. His name is William."

"William," he repeats, then rakes his hands tightly along his scalp before sitting down again. He mumbles something and I join him.

"Believe me, it's not serious," I say. "And that's usually what we argue about. We've never even...I mean, I've never *ever*..." But I stop, feeling too much like a complete dork to keep talking.

Robert's voice is soft and his eyes are like glass. "Do you want to be with him?"

This time I take his hands in mine. "No. Now that I know you're real—have always been real—there is nothing else but me and you. You have to know that."

He lets out a breath he's been holding. "Thank God," he whispers, looking like the weight of the universe just rolled off his chest.

"But I have to do the right thing by William, break it off with him as painlessly as possible. Can you understand that for me?"

Robert lifts my hand to his lips and whispers a warm kiss into my palm. Shivers consume me and goose bumps scatter my arms.

"You've always had such a big heart," he says. "And I do feel sorry for the guy." He gets a faraway look. "I know I'd be devastated if I lost you. My kindhearted, true-blue Anna."

"Yeah, well, I'm sure William won't feel the same way about my heart after I break his. I just wish you could've found me a few months ago before I ever met him."

"Me, too." He brushes a strand of hair from my face. "Because finding you sooner means loving you longer."

I want to kiss him so badly that it's hard to remember my loyalty to William, especially when I feel Robert's large hand find the small of my back and press a little. He leans in and whispers into my hair, "I have a confession to make. When you made the comment to me a little earlier about saying things to other girls, well there's only ever been one other girl, and that was in my first lifetime…before I met you."

"What? You mean—"

"I mean that after you, there's never been another woman for me."

I can't force down the lump in my throat. No way I'm holding it together now, not after such a sincere confession. I stand again, needing a little distance to quiet the voices now singing in my head. He's never been with another girl *after me*. But Robert's wrong about one thing. I'm not the one who's true-blue. No, that title securely belongs to him. My heart. My soul. My true-blue forever.

CHAPTER 6

Since leaving Robert's apartment, all I've managed is a little uneasy sleep on the end of the sofa. I stretch out a kink in my neck then look at my phone. Eleven-twenty. Not as late as I thought, thankfully. School's going to be brutal tomorrow, though. I feel like I haven't slept in a month. Or have I actually *been* asleep for a month. Did this happen? Is this real? Is my Robert truly in the present?

The smile that hasn't left my aching face lets me know he's very real, and for the first time in a long time, I'm happy. Not the *work-hard-and-you'll-finally-make-it* sort of happy, but the *I-actually-have-a-future-filled-with-hope* kind of happy. And it's nice. Freeing. Complicated? Absolutely. But for once, I have something to look forward to…and it feels good.

I check in on Mom before heading to my bedroom. She's snoring, so I don't go in. Last thing I want to do is wake her. I push my school books from my bed and climb under the cool sheets. As tired as I am after the most bizarre, wonderful day I've ever had in my life, I've been avoiding my bed. At first I thought I was just too crazy-rattled by seeing Robert, that I just couldn't settle down. But the longer I sat up on the couch watching trash TV and gorging myself on ice cream, the more I realized that my dream world has been my only comfort—my escape from Mom's drinking, from the ghosts of my dead family…from my life.

Turtles have shells that they carry around on their backs, tucking themselves securely inside at the first signs of danger. In that shell is their world. No one can pry them out, and no one is allowed in. That's what my dream world with Robert has been—my shell and safe haven. And now that he's here, I wonder if I'll ever see my dream world again, or if I'll even need it. He's here now, and that's all that matters. He's here…

The sun's shining high in the winter sky. Our barn's roof is whitewashed with snow, but it's stopped falling for now. Robert's taking advantage of the break to chop some firewood. I watch him from the porch as he swings the ax with his bare hands, his knuckles white as they grip the handle. He refuses to wear gloves, often reminding me that a craftsman needs the true sense of touch in order to create. I often remind him that frostbite makes no exception for an artist, but he's thickheaded.

Robert Jr. tugs the hem of my dress and I scoop him into my arms. "You'll catch your death out here, little one," I say, scurrying back inside the cabin with him.

"Pa," he says, pointing a tiny finger in Robert's direction as I close the door.

"Yes, that's Pa." I kiss his forehead and set him on a warm blanket in the kitchen near me, and I again stir the stew that's over the flame. I retrieve a paring knife from the pocket of my apron and chop another carrot into the pot. When the stew's thoroughly heated, I wipe my hands and pick my toddler up again. "Let's go see if Pa's finished with the wood so we can eat."

When I'm almost out the door, I see Robert standing a good distance from the house. He's talking to two men on horseback, but I can't see their faces clearly. Their voices are loud, then one of the men turns and rides away.

"You should have never brought him here!" Robert calls to the fleeing rider, who throws a hand into the air and rides away even faster. My stomach clenches. Something's dreadfully wrong.

Robert turns and runs toward the cabin. I step back, shielding Robert Jr. and myself with the partially opened door. When Robert's inside, he's practically panting. "Get Emily!" he says, his voice high and nasal.

"Who was that man?"

"There's no time," he says, placing the heavy wood block across the front door. "Just get the children and meet me at the back door. We have to make it to town and find the sheriff!"

Robert pulls his rifle down from above the mantel and heads to the door. I have both babies in my arms, but I stay in the bedroom when I hear a thundering voice I don't recognize.

"I told you not to let me find you, Grafton!" a man yells. "Now put the rifle down!"

Confusion hits me in the gut like a fist. A large man with a giant face and eyes that are too close together is standing in the back doorway, a pistol aimed at Robert's head. Who is this man, and why is he threatening my husband? Robert's eyes are wider than dinner plates, but he's not looking in my direction—obviously not wanting to draw attention to me and the children. Fear floods my brain like a pounding rain in a swollen gutter. What could my Robert have possibly done to make this man so angry? Would he really shoot him? I can't let this happen, but I'm too paralyzed with fear to react, unsure of what to do. I'm very aware that I'm helpless as the panic settles in.

The man steps closer to Robert. "You wouldn't consider a partnership with me, but word in town is that you're under contract with a man named Besson? Is that right?"

"We're not partners," Robert corrects. "I just make a few pieces of furniture a month and he sells them in his general store. That's all."

"That's quite enough!" the man yells. "Do you remember how handsomely I was willing to pay you for *a few pieces*? But no, my store wasn't good enough for your *masterpieces*, huh?"

"It had nothing to do with your store and you know it," Robert says. "I'm no one's puppet. And why do you care so much about me anyway, huh? Carpenters are readily accessible. You could have your pick of the lot."

"*You* were my pick of the lot! And I had buyers lined up, too. But you skipped town, left me looking like a fool." He holds the gun up higher, aiming squarely at Robert's forehead. "Well, no one tells me no, Grafton. No one."

Robert steps bravely forward. "So what are you going to do, Claude? Kill me because I wouldn't give you my furniture?"

"Give? I never expected you to give me your furn—"

"The entire town knew about your gambling problem! And the last guy who built for you didn't get paid for two winters. But somehow you coaxed him into working for you anyway. Tell me, Claude, what exactly did you use to persuade him? Your bullwhip, or your goons?"

The man smirks and my arms turn to gooseflesh. "I'll tell you what, Grafton. Hitch up your wagon with whatever pieces you have in the barn"—he glances around the room—"and in here, and we'll call it square."

Robert releases a breath he's been holding. "Agreed."

The man's smirks turn to raucous laughter. "Damn, Grafton. You're no fun anymore. No fun at all. What's made you all soft, huh?"

Fearing what's coming next, I whisper close to Robert Jr.'s ear, "Now just listen to Maw. We're going to play a little game. You must be very quiet. You mustn't make a single sound. If you do, you lose. But, if you are as quiet as a mouse, you win. Understand?"

My child's eyes tell me that he understands better than I credit him for. I set him on the bed and he looks at me with wide, desperate eyes. I place a sleeping Emily back in her cradle and position myself once again so I can see what's happening between my beloved and the monstrous man invading our home.

"You can have the furniture, Claude," Robert says. "Hell, I'll even give you an extra horse to help with the wagon. Just take what you want and go. No one has to know you were here. I won't go to the law. I give you my word."

"Ha! Your word? Your words are as useless as teats on a bull, Grafton. Keep your damn words." Claude picks up a blanket from the rocking chair and holds it to his nose, the gun never far from Robert's head. "Ah, so you have a woman, huh?" He inhales again. "And a child, I see." His smile is devilish. "Where are they?"

"In town," Robert lies. "And I would prefer for you to be gone when they return. I'll help you load the wagon. You can take whatever you want."

"Oh, never you mind that. I'll take what I want. How about I start with that right hand of yours, huh? We'll see how fine a craftsman you are without a hand."

I'm shaking so hard I can barely move as Robert pleads with the demon. Everything is flashing before my eyes as I stare into my husband's desperate face. Our courtship, wedding, the births of our babies, our life. I can't let anything happen to Robert, to our family. I have to do something. I place a hand on the front of my apron and remember the paring knife I have inside it. I glance about the room for one more item, then I turn to Robert Jr. I place a finger over my lips, reminding him to remain silent, then retrieve my music box with my left hand while keeping my other inside the apron around the knife.

"This will fetch a fine price," I say as I enter the common area.

"No, Anna! Run!" Robert begs. "Run now!"

I ignore his agonized pleas and keep talking. "It has a music-maker inside. It came all the way from France. It's a handsome piece, and Robert could make more. Here. You can have it."

"Well, looky here," Claude says. "How sweet. Come here, darlin'. Let me see that."

Robert bolts forward as I step closer, but Claude points the gun at my head instead, and he stops. "Please don't hurt her!"

"Back away, Grafton, or your pretty little wife won't be pretty much longer!"

Robert puts his hands in the air and slowly backs up. "Fine, I'll do whatever you say. Just don't hurt her."

"Now, come here, darlin'," Claude says again. "Let me see that trinket of yours."

I look into Robert's desperate eyes, a sudden rush of cold crossing my face. I want to cry out, yell at the monster in front of me to disappear, but the sounds in my head evaporate like dew on the leaves, useless and unspoken. "Here, see for yourself," I manage instead and hand him my music box.

Claude leaves the gun aimed in my direction, glancing from me to Robert to the box. When his attention is more on the music box than his captives, I nod to Robert and pull the knife from my apron. Together, we push toward Claude. But we're not fast enough. Claude fires a shot in Robert's direction, then pulls me into his body. My music box drops to the floor, and Claude twists the knife from my grasp. The gun is lodged under my chin as the giant man holds me with little effort. He has my knife in his other hand. An unscathed Robert freezes and I cry out, tears flooding my cheeks.

"Back away, Grafton!" the giant yells. "I'll kill her, I swear it!"

"Kill me instead," Robert says. "That's what you came here for, right?"

The baby is crying now, and my soul aches to comfort

her. But there's little I can do, and I know it. Panic fills me in every crevice of my being, but I'm motionless. The barrel of the gun is pushing into my flesh, but all I can think about is Robert. Our babies. Our life together.

Claude says the words against my cheek as I'm motionless in front of him. "You know, I had a wife too. Beautiful, like this one. But she left me. Said she was tired of the drinking and the gambling, but I know the real reason. It was because I lost the store. You were my last shot at keeping my business, Grafton. But, you were too good to work for me, huh? And because of you, I lost everything. And now you're going to lose everything, too."

I hear Robert's screams as he lunges forward, everything around me slowing to a crawl. I await the thunderous sound of the gun, but instead feel a burning across my neck, the pain so great I can barely scream. I grab my neck, blood pouring through my fingers like water from the river as I fall to the floor. The giant is running away now and Robert is at my side in seconds, his hands covering my opened neck. I realize the irony—the giant has slit my throat with my own cooking knife. Robert's screaming, first my name, then for God to help him. My vision's fading. I hear gurgling and realize it's coming from me. I can't breathe. I search Robert's face. He's saying he loves me. I can no longer support the weight of my head. It falls to the side and I see Robert Jr. standing in the doorway of the bedroom. Still silent. So silent...

I awaken when the darkness fully consumes me, still clutching my neck and gasping for breath. I'm panicking, can't seem to get enough air. I stand, willing my lungs to take in breaths, reminding myself that I'm no longer in the wilderness. My thoughts scatter like rain over water. Oh my God. Robert watched that man kill me. But why...? I touch my neck. No wonder it's always hurt to be touched. It was severed in my other lifetime. "I was murdered," I whisper. "Murdered…" When another thought enters my racing brain, I grab my keys and head for the door. It's raining, but I don't care. I have to go to him…

***

Robert swings the door to his apartment open after I pound on it several times. "Oh my God, Anna. You're soaked to the bone. What're you doing here? Get inside."

I'm shivering from the rain, but I don't budge. "Am I dying?"

"What?" Robert says, confusion twisting his face.

I touch my neck. "Is that why you're here? Because I'm going to die?"

CHAPTER 7

I focus on the buzzing in my ears. It's louder than everything else around me—louder than the rain, the random cars pulling into the apartment complex, Robert's voice.

"Please come in, Anna," he pleads once more. "We need to talk. You can't just stand out here all night letting water ping you in the head, can you?"

But maybe that's *exactly* what I need—for the rain to wash away the nightmare still possessing my mind and body, to wash away the ruins of the past. But I don't protest when I feel his hands on my arms, tugging me inside with him. Robert grabs a blanket from the back of the couch and drapes it over my shoulders.

"Are you cold?"

I'm so cold it feels like my bones are shifting in my skin, but I don't care. There's only one thing I need now, only one thing I came for. Answers. "I need to know why you're really here. What are you not telling me, Robert? Are you here because I'm going to die?"

His expression softens and I see confusion in his face. "No, of course not. Why would you ever think that? What happened that has you so upset?"

"I had another dream of our life in the wilderness, and a man slit my throat. He slit my throat, and then I died."

"Oh God, Anna. I'm so sorry—"

"And not only that, but I *felt* it, too. The pain, the not being able to breathe. And you were screaming. Robert Jr. was there, all wide-eyed and quiet. Look, you had no time to tell me then, so tell me now. Who was that man and why did he kill me?"

He lowers his head as though my words just punched him. After several seconds, he takes my hand and leads me to the couch. "Now you know why it's so hard for me to look at you without wanting to hold you," he says. "You were so brutally taken from me. I've replayed that day in my head a million times. What I could have done to stop it, what I *should* have done. But deep down, I know I did the best I could. We both did the best we thought we could that day, but it wasn't enough. Is never enough…"

When thunder claps so ferociously his walls seem to shake our heads turn in the direction of the window. His eyes meet mine again.

"You're shivering. Wait a second. I'll be right back."

"But, Robert…" I don't realize until this moment that he's shirtless. I watch his bare back almost sprint down the short hallway. I take a few deep breaths in an effort to calm my exploding nerves, and rub my arms to warm them. He returns a minute later wearing a shirt, and he tosses something in my direction.

"They'll be way too big but a lot warmer than what you're wearing now." It's one of his T-shirts and a pair of drawstring athletic shorts. He's matter-of-fact. "You don't need to stay in those wet clothes."

I inch the blanket from my shoulders and look down at my rain-soaked pink cami and white boy shorts, knowing full-well he's gotten an eyeful. My cheeks now match the cami. I'll probably catch pneumonia as a result of my panic. "You must think I'm insane," I whisper.

He smiles. "Frightened, yes. Insane, no."

"Would you mind?" I motion for him to look away so I can take advantage of his offer.

"Oh, yeah. Sure."

Quickly, I slip out of my wet clothes and into his shirt and shorts, chills still consuming me, but for an entirely different reason. "Thank you. I'm decent now."

He faces me again and we return to the couch. Robert insists that I keep the blanket around me and I don't argue.

"Now tell me," I say again, "why did that man slit my throat? Who was he?"

It's obvious that the subject is more than a delicate one for him. At first he searches my eyes, as if he needs to know I'll still be here after his explanation. The muscles in his jaw twitch and his eyes are glassed with tears. He pulls a hand over his scalp, his sun-touched curls still glorious even with bedhead.

"His name was Claude Adams," he says. "He owned a general store two towns north of our settlement. I lived there briefly while I was searching for you. When I finally happened upon you at the river that day, I never returned north. Had no reason to. Claude had been trying to persuade me to make furniture for his store, but I kept refusing. He had a reputation of being cruel. Everyone knew his store was just a front for gambling and drinking in the back storeroom after hours. I wanted no part of that. When he found our cabin that day, well..."

"I know the rest," I say, trying to relieve him from retelling my fate.

"I've always blamed myself for your death." He cups my cheek and speaks just above a whisper. "Claude wanted to take the one thing I treasured most...blamed me for what was his own doing. Well, when he took you from me, he succeeded. I was crushed beyond measure."

I recoil from him a little and he notices. "What happened to him? After he killed me, I mean. Did he just get away with it?"

Roberts stares at me for several seconds. His hand

finds my cheek again and smolders against my skin. "No, my sweet Anna, he didn't get away with it. He was hanged three days later. A lynch mob hunted him down two days after you were buried."

"A lynch mob? Why?"

Robert's hand trails from my cheek, down my neck and finally rests over my heart. "Why? Because of this. You have the sweetest soul, Anna. The kindest heart I've ever known. Everyone in town loved you. I never had to call for justice. Justice was freely given. They left him hanging from the town gallows for a week until he resembled the monster he truly was."

We're silent for a moment then Robert adds, "Listen, I'm not here because you're dying or because I know some grand, master plan for our lives. Like I said before, we're the only ones repeating. You don't have to worry about that son-of-a-bitch who killed you back then ever touching you again. Understand?"

"That's just it," I say. "I don't understand. How are we here? Why are we repeating?"

"I don't know," Robert says, "but I do know that I want to be a better man for you. I never should have let Claude get that close to you...should've stopped him from getting in the cabin in the first place. But he'll never hurt you again. You don't have to carry those scars with you—"

"But I do hold a scar. My neck has always hurt to be touched. I never understood why...until tonight."

"Oh, Anna. I'm so sorry." He trails a finger across my neck, the sensation a little painful at first, but then bearable. He covers my neck fully with his hand, as though he's trying to extract the very poison that took my life two hundred years ago. "Your neck is perfect, you know that?"

"Well, it's a little scrawny. I wouldn't say it's perfect."

"I want to kiss you. Right here, right now."

I'm caught off guard, but I want to kiss him too, more than anything else in the world.

"Would you allow me to kiss you? I mean, I know you

think you have an obligation to what's his name? William? Do you want me to kiss you?"

"I've wanted you to kiss me since the first night I dreamed of you."

He's not looking at me but his hand is on mine, his index finger making what feels like eyelash touches on the top of my hand. It almost tickles, but I don't dare move.

"I won't kiss you unless you ask me to," he says again.

I try holding back a smile, but he notices.

"What?"

"I recall you telling me once upon a time that I'd never have to ask to be kissed."

He leans into me before I finish the words, his hand behind the back of my neck before it rests fully on the couch pillow. A soft heat captures my lips when his mouth meets mine, his warmth quickly spreading through my whole body. For a moment I forget to breathe, but it's okay. I don't need air. I realize that I'm never more alive than when I'm in his arms.

He whispers against my lips, "I'll never let anyone hurt you again. I swear it."

I was wrong. He is the air, and the sky. He is space and time. He's every escape I've ever needed. Every prayer when I thought there were none left to pray. And when his mouth finds mine again, I'm home. I don't know how long we kiss, but when he finally pulls away from me, I miss him already. He was right. The firsts are always the best.

"It's late," he says. "Has to be after two. What if your mom wakes up?"

"She'll freak. I know, I know. I need to go."

He wraps his arms around me again and then walks me to the door. Fortunately, the rain's stopped. He's still watching me as I step into my car. I give him a slight nod and pull out of the parking space. As I head toward home, I wonder if I'll ever dream of our wilderness days again. So far, every dream I've ever had was in a sequence—us meeting, our courtship, our wedding, our babies, and now

I've seen my death. What is there after death? Then I smile. This, this is what's after death. My life with Robert all over again.

***

When I finally make it home, I turn the key as quietly as possible in the front door and tiptoe inside. I pass Mom's door and she's still snoozing away. Thank God she sleeps like a hibernating bear most of the time. I close my bedroom door behind me, letting out a breath I've been holding since sneaking back in like a creeper. I realize that I never grabbed my phone when I left for Robert's. There are three text messages from William. Guilt hits me as I read his sincere comments, how he can't sleep and is nervous about his first football game tomorrow night. As much as I wanted to break it off with him in the morning, I know I can't do it until after the game. I'd never want to be the reason he didn't perform well. I'm going to hurt him bad enough as it is. I can at least give him that.

I climb under the covers again, now draped in Robert's shirt. I pull it to my nose and inhale his scent. When sleep finds me once more, I'm safe and happy.

CHAPTER 8

It doesn't take a lot of convincing to persuade Maggie to come to William's game with me. She says she hated all the "Maggie the Jaggie" references she got last year at our own football games anyway, but I know the truth. She thinks William might have some hot friends he can introduce her to after the game, and that's perfectly fine with me. She can think whatever she wants as long as I have her as a buffer between me and Will tonight. I'm Maggie's ride, so I won't have to be alone with him. And I can call him in the morning and simply say I don't think we should see each other anymore. The old *it's not you, it's me*. Cowardly, but effective—at least that's how I'm choosing to view it. I just don't think I could stand hurting him like that in person. I just hope he takes it okay.

"These bleachers sure aren't very comfortable." Maggie points to a couple of ladies beside us. "If we're gonna do this every Friday night, we need to get some of those cushion thingys like they have."

"Yeah, well, do you suggest we get the *same* ones they have, or buy ones with *our* school's mascot on it?"

She rolls her eyes. "Ha ha. You're real funny, but kinda harsh."

"No, seriously, you sure you wouldn't rather be at our game?" I ask again just because I feel like I should. And because this will be the last game I attend at Central…ever.

Maggie flips a blonde curl away from her shoulder. "Let's see, would I rather be at Northridge or here? If I had to guess, at our school right about now Ms. Eckhart has caught every sociology student at the entrance and forced them to pass around her petition on violence in video games, and every guy at our school with a heartbeat is willingly taking a clipboard just to get a good look at her cleavage. You know that's why she wears everything so low-cut, right? To make the boys do her dirty work? Well, I'm not getting signatures for her or whatever the hell it is she needs."

"What's all that petition stuff about anyway?" I try sounding more interested than I really am.

"It's her own personal deal. She's going to night school to get her Master's degree or something. If you ask me, she's just a big ol' cheater. Should be getting her own stupid signatures."

I nod. "Agreed."

Maggie squirms on the uncomfortable bleachers some more, accidentally bumping my elbow for the zillionth time. "So what number is William?"

"Number five."

She eyes the sidelines. "Wow, he's tall. Looks more like a basketball player if you ask me."

Central High is ahead when the second quarter starts, thanks to two field goals by William. I'm glad he's doing so well considering I'm breaking up with him tomorrow. He'll have no problem finding another girlfriend, especially now that he's proving to be a football god. That's the one thing you can count on in Alabama. Football is a vast kingdom, and if you're decent at it, you're royalty.

"You hungry?" I ask Maggie when I notice her eyeing a girl's nachos.

"A little. You going to the concession stand?"

"Yeah, I'm thirsty."

"Come here." She wriggles a finger near my face so I'll lean in to her. "You know, Dalton Sellers said that if you go to the back of Central's concession stand near the bathrooms, there's this guy who always wears a red stocking cap who'll sell you a fake ID for fifty bucks. I wonder if it's true?"

I snicker. "Doubtful. What the hell do you need a fake ID for anyway? You don't even drink."

She flips her hair away from her face. "Well, I'm thinking about trying it."

"Why?" I cut her a look and she wrinkles her nose.

"Same reason I joined the debate team last year. Boredom. Uber, massive boredom."

I shake my head and stand. "Trust me, keep on debating and just leave the fake ID guy standing alone at the bathrooms. Alcohol consumption's not the answer for boredom."

"Oh yeah? Well, who died and left you the expert on the subject, huh?"

My dad and sister. But I don't say it, just simply reiterate, "No fake ID and no alcohol. But I got you covered on the nachos."

"Party pooper," she mutters.

"Twisted," I mutter right back and she laughs. "I better go before halftime starts or it'll be so crowded I'll miss most of third quarter. You coming?"

"No, I'll save our seats." She hands me a five. "Think that'll be enough for nachos and a drink?"

I fish in my purse for a ten-spot I know is in there somewhere. When I feel my lipstick tube instead, I pull it out and smooth some over my chapped lips.

"Oh, I want some."

I hand the lipstick to Maggie then retrieve the ten. "Be right back."

The concession stand is already pretty crowded when I join the line. I pull out my phone and try talking low enough that no one will hear me. "Hey, Mom. Thought I'd check in on you while I have a minute. You okay?"

"Anna, baby. Yeah, I'm fine. Don't worry about me. Just go on and have fun with your friends."

I gauge how much she's already had to drink by the amount of time it takes her to answer the phone, and if her words sound slurred at all. No slurring yet, but it took five rings. She's well on her way. "Please don't drink too much, Mom. I won't be real late. I promise."

Several kids eye me suspiciously like they know I go to Northridge or something. It makes me fidget and wrap the front of my arms tightly around my middle, even though I'm not cold in the slightest. Honestly, I couldn't care less what they think of me, I just hate the staring. Rudeness is a very unattractive quality. But when I notice a girl make a tunnel around her friend's ear and glare at me like I'm a supervillain, I figure all the attention has everything to do with William and nothing to do with me. Somehow they know I'm the *outsider* he's dating. Well, that won't be an issue much longer. I look away, choosing to ignore their ridiculousness instead.

I reach in my purse and trail a finger along the edge of the card Robert wrote his info on. I know it's silly, but having it with me makes me feel closer to him. I can't help but wonder what he's doing tonight. It's funny, but when Robert was solely in my dream world, I had patience in spades. No dreams of us for a month, six months? It was okay because I knew more would eventually follow. Sure, I longed for him every single day and missed our life together more than air, but I could wait for the dreams. Now that I know he's here, flesh-and-bone and wanting me as much as I want him, I've never craved anything or anyone so badly. And as soon as I set things right with William, nothing in this life or the next will keep me from my Robert.

When it's finally my turn after the crazy-long wait, I order the food and head back to the bleachers. Maggie's handing a phone back to a girl in a group sitting a row above us.

"You know," she says, "I feel like that nerd who just gets asked to take the pictures but never gets asked to be in them. Be honest with me, Anna. Am I that nerd? Just tell me…" She takes a deep breath and then lets it out. "I can take it."

I burst out laughing. "You're *seriously* deranged, you know that?"

"What I am is seriously bored," she corrects. "Now hand me that grub."

***

I'm waiting outside the field house for William. Central won, thank goodness. Maggie's in the restroom. I told her to hurry but that girl never listens. I really want her here with me when Will comes out. I'm tapping my foot and looking in the direction of the restrooms when I spot someone and nearly run to him without thinking. I take in a breath. I never told him that William goes to this school, or that I would be at the game, for that matter. So why is Robert here?

"So, are you going to say hello?" he asks when he joins me. "And you look beautiful, by the way. I like your hair like that."

I reach up and readjust the pearl comb that's holding one side of my hair in place. I say through the smile that's sticking to my teeth, "I *should* say hello, but what I really want to know is what you're doing here."

"Just thought I'd take in a high school game, and I heard Central's kicker is pretty good." He winks.

"Now you're just messing with me." But I smile straight through the panic. "This is too weird. Look, William will be out soon and you can't be here. Seriously, Robert, what're you doing?"

He sighs. "Okay look, you're right. I shouldn't be here,

73

but I was worried. I know you're breaking up with him and just want you to be okay. I mean, do I have to worry about this guy doing something stupid when you give him the news? Look, I can follow you if I need to. He'll never know I'm there. I can be very subtle."

The earthy scent swirling around him reminds me of our past life, and the peppered stubble on his tightened jaw has my knees weak. One thing's certain—nothing about Robert Grafton is subtle. "How did you know he played for Central, anyway?"

"Facebook."

Figures. "Oh, so you were stalking my Facebook again, huh?"

He fumbles for a moment. "Well…yeah…but I wasn't trying to be a creeper or anything. I was just…concerned."

"Oh my Lord, I'm teasing you. I know your intentions, but I'm fine. My friend's in the restroom and she'll be out any second. I'll call you tomorrow, okay?"

His eyes soften and search mine like he's looking for reassurance. "Remember what we talked about last night? It's just that I've carried around so much guilt for so long. I can't ever let you get hurt again…not ever."

He trails a finger across my throat, and the pain in his eyes makes any discomfort I've ever felt in my neck seem petty and small. The pain my murder caused him is obviously unrelenting, and his eyes make me wonder how he's carried such a burden all these years. I want to hold him until the hurt dissolves, until my breath is all he feels—until he knows above all else that I'm alive, safe.

And that for however many forevers we're given, I'm his.

But for now I simply grasp his hand. "William's harmless. And besides, in this life I can take care of myself. Trust me, I've had lots of practice."

His smile lets me know he doesn't doubt my competence in the slightest. "I'm sure you can. Just be extra careful."

I let go of his hand when I see Maggie near the field house doors again and nudge him in the opposite direction. "That's my friend. You have to go now."

As he's walking away, I hear the words, "'Til the morrow, my love."

When he speaks to me like *my Robert*, all I want to do is follow him. But I have to see this through—have to set things right with William or I'd never be able to live with myself. So I head in Maggie's direction without looking back.

"What up, Buttercup?" she says when I'm within earshot. "Looks like some of the other players are finally coming out. How much longer do you think he'll be?"

"Not a clue." I let out a breath, relieved she apparently didn't see me with Robert. "But I doubt he'll be much longer." I can tell she touched up her lips with my lipstick again. My shade looks better on her than me. Think I'll let her keep it.

"Hey, Anna." William kisses me on the cheek and I throw a hand to my nose without thinking.

"I know. I stink. Sorry."

"It's okay." I turn to Maggie. "This is my friend. I've told you about her. Maggie, this is William."

"Nice to meet you." Maggie's eager with a handshake and William obliges, but then turns to me. "I thought we'd go out tonight, celebrate my win. Is your friend gonna be with us the whole time?"

I glance in Maggie's direction. "Don't be rude, Will. I invited Maggie so I wouldn't have to watch the game alone. And it's not exactly like you're dressed for us to go out anyway, so what difference does it make?"

Maggie holds her nose. "Yeah, dude. You smell like two gallons of sweat. Where were you planning on taking Anna, anyway? The weight room?" She snickers at her wit, and William's jaw tightens.

"Not exactly." He looks at me and I force a smile.

"Oh, hang on a minute. I think I know that girl."

Maggie bolts toward a brunette a few feet away and starts chattering like a bird in a tree.

"Talkative girl." William drops his gym bag and nods to a couple of players exiting the field house.

"Yeah, and you'd like her if you'd be nice to her for five minutes."

"Well, what I really wish is that one of my friends would like her so she'd catch a ride with one of them."

Maggie would love nothing more, but it's not happening. No way is he dismantling my buffer zone that easily. "I'm not letting my friend get in a car with some strange guy she's only known for two minutes. Forget it."

His expression softens. "I know. I was just kidding. But I really wanted some alone time with you tonight. I feel like we barely see each other anymore."

I wish by some miracle William would lose his patience and his interest in me right here, right now—tell me I'm a sucky girlfriend and that we should start seeing other people. But instead he looks at me with anguished eyes— eyes that would make any other girl pull him close to her and smother him with kisses until the hurt dulled. But I'm not that girl. So I'm more than grateful when Maggie rejoins us.

"Sorry to walk off like that," she says, "but I went to middle school with that chick."

"No biggie," I assure her then turn my attention to William again. "So, what's the plan?"

"Well, I rode to school with Mike today. I mean, I knew you were coming tonight and would have your car, and I didn't want us to be dealing with separate vehicles—"

"So it looks like we're taking the Blue Wombat," Maggie says. "Let's head."

William reaches around for his bag, and one of his teammates slaps his shoulder. "Awesome game, Hull. You the man."

"Thanks, dude. Hey, Kurt, this is my girlfriend Anna.

And this is her friend Maggie. Ladies, this is Kurt."

"Nice to meet you," Kurt says. "I'm a running back."

"Yeah, well, he needs to run back to wherever he came from," Maggie says into my ear when William and Kurt start talking amongst themselves about the game.

"Yeah, well, you better make that clear with Will, then. I think he wants to pawn you off on that dude so he can be alone with me."

"Gross," Maggie replies. "I'm not going anywhere with that guy. He stinks worse than William. No offense."

"None taken. I told him not to, but he seems pretty determined."

We look in the guys' direction again and it's obvious that William is asking Kurt about the Maggie situation. "Nope, not happening," Maggie says. "If I'm gonna be auctioned off to the highest bidder, then it's time to do my own picking."

"It's not like that," I say, but Maggie ignores me. She eyes the people walking past and coos when she sees Robert.

Oh God!

"Ask William if he knows *him*. If I have to make myself scarce, it can at least be with someone hot." Maggie's watching Robert's every move, and I'm frozen. She nudges my arm. "Hurry up and ask him before he gets away."

I blurt out before thinking, "He doesn't know him."

"Really? How would you know? They obviously go to the same school—"

"No, that guy's in college—"

"So you're saying *you* know him?" Maggie's practically drooling.

"Well, yeah, but—"

"Even better." She heads in Robert's direction before I can stop her. *Crap...*

I stare at Maggie as she shakes Robert's hand, her smile so big it could light up the world. He's graced my lips with that same smile by looking at me, has snared me in those gentle, caramel eyes more times than I can recall. But the fire those eyes normally kindle in my belly are now scorching my insides like a blowtorch. Maggie's gushing over my Robert, and before logic can coax me not to be, I'm jealous.

She takes Robert's arm, pulling him to the front of the field house with her. "Look who I found," she announces when she's in front of me again.

I can feel my face flaming red so I don't look in William's direction. I wrap my arms around Robert's neck instead. "Oh my gosh. It's been such a long time! How've you been?"

"Fine," he says, playing it cooler than Alaska in winter. "How 'bout yourself? Wow, Anna. It's been a while."

A dejected Kurt leaves, and William's at my side when the hug's barely over. "Hey, man, what's up?"

"Not too much," Robert says. "Hey, you're the kicker for Central, right? Outstanding job tonight."

Sometimes I forget how smooth he can be.

"Thanks," Will replies, the flattery relieving some of the tightness in his face. "William Hull."

"Robert Grafton."

"So," Will says, "you and Anna know each other, huh?"

"We do," Robert says. "Anna and I go way back."

My knees threaten to buckle, but I manage to keep my composure.

"You go to Northridge, then?" Will asks.

"No. I'm a—"

"He's a freshman at Bama," Maggie says. "Hey, I have an idea. Why don't I get Robert to take me home so you two lovebirds can be alone? Anna and I can hang out any time."

Robert grits his teeth and shoves his hands in his pockets at the word *lovebirds*, as though if he doesn't remove those large, masterful hands from the situation they'll simply scoop me up and whisk me away with him. I cut my eyes at Maggie, but she's oblivious—too caught up in Robert's beauty to notice my disapproval. Can't really blame her, but that doesn't keep me from wanting to strangle her right now.

"I think that sounds awesome," William says. "That way, everybody's happy."

No, that way *he's* happy. Oh, and Maggie. She's no doubt crazy outrageously fantastically happy.

"You don't have a problem with that, do you, Anna?" Maggie's practically floating, and my stomach's twisting in so many knots it feels like putty.

"No, I don't have a problem with that."

Robert gives me a slight nod and hint of a smile. He knows the deal, but so do I. My buffer is leaving with my heart, and now I have to face William alone.

CHAPTER 9

William and I are in my car way too soon, driving down the road toward his house so he can shower and change. I know what I need to say, but I'm not sure how to start the conversation. I need some time to think, to find the words that won't simply crush his heart and leave him wondering where we went wrong. But I'll never be afforded the time, because as much as I want to spare him pain, the selfish part of my heart can't stop thinking about Maggie and Robert.

What's happening between them this very moment? Is she whispering in his ear as he's driving, lightly brushing his hand and making it seem like an accident? Is she tracing a finger along the small line of curls on the back of his neck, causing the goose bumps he always gets on his arms when he's touched there? Is she giggling at the cute expression he makes when he's trying to tell a joke just right—consumed by his every word and hoping her bold flirting will be enough to make him ask her out? My mind's running rampant and my insides are twisting. As much as I care about Maggie, I don't want her thinking she has a chance with Robert. So I tug my mind free from those thoughts and focus on the matter at hand. I have to talk to

William, get this over with once and for all.

"So," Will says right as I'm about to open my mouth, "that Robert guy, how do you know him?"

I hope he can't see how red my cheeks feel. "Like he said, we go way back."

"But you've known Maggie for a while too, right?"

"Yeah, what's your point?"

"It's just that she didn't seem to know him. If you've been friends with Maggie for years and you and this Robert dude go way back, how come they've never met?"

I hate lying to him, but I refuse to be interrogated when it comes to Robert. He's my hot-button topic and my objectivity is slipping by the second. "Because he and his family moved to South Carolina, but now he's back here going to school. Why do you care so much, anyway?"

"Trust me, I don't. It just seemed weird, that's all. And besides, there's nothing wrong with me asking about a guy who was hugging all up on my girl, now is there?"

His hand finds my knee and I squirm. "Well, how many times have I ever asked you about girls you might be friends with at your school, huh? How about never."

He frowns. "Oh, I ask about this Robert dude and now I can't touch your knee. Fine, then."

I ignore the question, but he moves his hand anyway, obviously agitated. And I can't say that I blame him. Thank God we're on his street. I pull into his driveway and look at him after I turn off the car.

"William, we need to talk."

"Oh God, what is it now? I put my hand on your knee. Big deal. We can't really be in a relationship if you never want me to touch you or ask you a single question, can we?"

The words come out sounding more timid than I want them to. "No, actually we can't."

"Good. I'm glad you see it my way." He winks, but when he notices my expression, his eyes search mine. "Something's wrong. What is it, Anna? Please tell me. I was asking you a question. That's all, I swear. What's wrong?"

How do I explain, ever make him understand that for years now I've only been half a person—always knowing that somewhere in the universe my other half was waiting. That even if that other half was in another lifetime, he was real and the slightest essence of him has always been enough to keep me from ever really loving anyone but him. How do I make William understand that my heart has never really been free to love him?

I push the words out. "I don't think we should see each other anymore."

His face is like stone and his words are sharp and strained. "What do you mean? This is crazy! What did I do?"

"You didn't do anything. Honestly, William. It's not you, it's me." I hate the clichéd words the moment they leave my mouth, but it doesn't make them any less true. Nothing about this break-up has anything to do with Will, and I hate it.

"But a couple of days ago you changed your relationship status to being in a relationship with *me*. I thought that meant things were good between us, moving forward. Haven't I been patient, Anna? Have I ever pushed you to do anything you didn't want to do?"

"Well, no. Not really—"

"Not ever!" It startles me when he yells, and I draw back a little. "I never forced you," he says. "Never."

"Well, I did have to ask you to slow down a few times when you were moving a little fast for me," I remind him, not because it bothered me to slow him down, but because he's yelling and I'm lashing out.

"When we were moving *too fast*? Damn, Anna. We never moved fast. All we ever did was barely creep along. All you ever wanted me to do was sniff around your skirt and beg."

His words cut like a biting rain, but I know it's because

he's hurt—can't possibly understand any of this. "I never wanted you to beg," I say. "That's why this is over. I think you should go now before you say something you don't mean."

I can tell he's holding back tears, and his intensity scares me a little. But that is the one thing I learned about William early on—he's very serious when it comes to dating, and he fell for me pretty quickly. I expected him to be hurt, but he's more emotional than I ever anticipated. So I'm definitely not expecting it when he cups my face.

"What can I do to prove that I'm the right guy for you? You're my girl. Just give me a chance. Deep down, you have to know how I feel about you. My Anna—"

I'm resolute when I move his hands. "But I'm not your girl, William."

Humiliation races across his face as he fumbles for the door handle. "Yeah, I guess you never were." His eyes are glassed with tears when he opens the car door. He slams it so hard I fear the Wombat may lose an appendage, but I let it go. He's hurt and I feel bad, but I know it was the only way.

As I watch William head toward his front door, I'm reminded of the old cliché of fireworks exploding when lovers kiss, as if the fireworks are the magic in the moment itself. But that reference couldn't be further from the truth. William's pain is a better representation of fireworks, exploding desperately into a darkened sky, aching to reach the dimmest spot in my heart and illuminate it with his love. But he's in the wrong place, the wrong sky, no matter how magnificent his colors may prove to be. He's unable to light my soul, to sway my heart. He's instead reduced to swirls of smoke in the pitch of night.

I just hope one day he finds his sky.

***

I had to force myself to resist calling Robert at least a

dozen times before I got home, reminding myself that it wouldn't be the smartest thing to do if he was still with Maggie. Mom's passed out in her bed when I check on her. I can always tell when she's passed out, as opposed to simply sleeping, by the way she's positioned on the bed.

She hasn't had a sober weekend in two months now, and I wonder how long she can keep this up. The thought of coming home and finding her dead crosses my mind for the thousandth time, but I push it down—so far down in my mind that I hope it stays buried. No way I can lose my mom, too. And I know what's coming next, no matter how hard I try convincing myself that it'll be different this time. No sober weekends will soon turn to drinking during the week and missing work. Hopefully she'll stop herself before she uses up the vacation days she's been saving. I need to convince her to go to rehab. We can't keep this up.

I lift her head as gently as possible and place a pillow underneath it. "Is that better, Mom?" I whisper. She sighs and I lie next to her, ignoring her stale, sweaty smell to hug her close.

"I broke up with William tonight. He's a decent guy, but he's not the one."

I know she can't hear me, but I need to talk to her, craving mother-daughter time even if it's fake. I'll take whatever I can get.

"Do you know *how* I know William's not the one? Because Robert's here. You've always hated me talking about my wilderness dreams, but it's different now. Robert's real, and he's in Tuscaloosa. How wild is that?" I grin when the corny but perfect phrasing hits me. "Mom, he's the man of my dreams."

She whimpers, and I kiss her cheek. My throat tightens but I hold the tears inside, like I have for too long now. I know she's broken, but I wish somehow she could see how much her drinking breaks the both of us. I say the words close to her ear.

"So listen, Mom. We have to get you better so you can meet him, okay? You'll love Robert. I know you will. We need to get you back in rehab. The sooner the better." I brush her hair away from her face before standing. "I'll let you sleep in peace now. I love you, Mom."

I close her door as quietly as possible and head to my own room. I pull my phone from my pocket. He should've had Maggie home by now. I touch Robert's name and wait for the rings.

"Hey, Anna." His velvety voice melts me. "I'm so glad it's you. How'd it go?"

"He didn't take it too well, but it's done. I'm just glad it's over. And I'm sure he'll be fine in a few days."

"You'll never know how relieved I am."

I change the subject to what's been running through my mind more than anything. "So how'd it go with Maggie? I know she can be kind of...*forward*."

"Oh, Maggie? She's still here. Wanna talk to her?"

"What—?"

"Just kidding."

I let out the breath I've been holding. "That was mean!"

He's snickering. "No, that was funny. Maggie was trying really hard, but I told her I'm seeing someone."

I close my eyes, listening to the familiar voice I know better than my own as he rambles about taking Maggie home. I still can't believe he's here, that we're free to be together. I pinch the arm that's holding my phone and smile at the hint of pain. I push the phone tighter against my ear, loving his voice, the breath I hear him take when he's silent. The anxiety from earlier eases away, and I'm content just listening to him.

"So, all that aside, there's something I want to ask you," he says.

"What's that?"

"Will you go out with me tomorrow night?"

"You're asking me out...on a date?" I rub the tingles

from my arms. "We still have a lot to talk about, you know. I have so many questions. I'd really be fine just going to your apartment—"

"I know, I know," he says, "and I'll answer all your questions the best I can. But first I want to take you out on a date. I think we deserve a little fun. Don't you?"

No way I'm arguing with that logic. "Sounds amazing."

"Great. I'll pick you up around six, then. How does dinner and dancing sound?"

"Dinner sounds fabulous, but I'm afraid I'm not a very good dancer."

"I know, but I'll teach you. After all, I've taught you to dance in every lifetime."

I feel the tears before they touch my cheeks. "Really?"

"Really, my sweet Anna. Like I said, lots of firsts. So, I'll see you tomorrow evening then?"

"You will."

"Good night, Anna."

"Good night."

I fall onto my bed, every image I've ever had of Robert swirling through my head at once. Seeing Robert at the lake for the first time. Robert asking me to marry him. Our wedding day. The day our son was born. The day our daughter was born. Our cabin in the wilderness in the dead of winter, stoking a fire with wood chopped with his strong, massive hands. Those same hands holding our babies. Those hands holding me. Then seeing Robert in the mall, the shock that ripped through me like a razor when I realized he was mine and he was here.

But not once do I ever remember dancing...

CHAPTER 10

"Wow, that *was* quite the pickle," Rose says. "So, is there any way William or Maggie could know that Robert is your beau? I mean, your true beau?"

"My *only* beau," I correct. "And, no. There's no way. I've never shared my wilderness dreams with Maggie. And no way was I ever telling William about them, even if Robert hadn't shown up in this lifetime. I'm just glad it's over—between me and Will, I mean. The last thing I wanted to do was hurt him."

Rose gets a faraway look—a look I recognize—so I let her sit while I thumb through the few remaining charts of the other residents I still have to visit in a little while. She's having one of her "fretful mornings", as New York would describe it, and it breaks my heart. Most days Rose is as lucid as me, can tell you what she wore to church on Easter Sunday when she was four. Other days, she can't recall what she had for breakfast. Bad Saturday mornings like this one remind me that she's old, and I just want to stop time—keep her here and healthy forever.

I add more butter to her grits when I realize she's barely touched them and nudge her tray a little closer to her. "I can walk you to the cafeteria if you'd rather eat there," I remind her. "You can be with people instead of in this room, looking at the same four walls. And I'll sit with you too if you want. It's no biggie."

"I would've given anything to be there with you last night, Anna. Anything."

Her hazy stare worries me, and I place a hand on top of hers. "At a high school football game? Why?"

"I bet that was a sight to behold," she says, ignoring my question, filling the room with her voice like she has to keep talking to simply exist. "I would've liked to have seen you with them. Bet that was a hoot." She stares out the window again. "I want to meet him...your Robert."

"You will. I promise."

Her eyes are watery, but she's not crying. She looks older than I've ever noticed, and it scares me. She turns her whole body to face me. "But you have to break it off with William, in a proper way. It's only right."

My heart sinks. "I already did, after the football game last night. I told you about it. Remember?"

"Oh yes, that's right. I would've given anything to be there last night, Anna. Anything..."

I take a deep breath to relieve the sudden tightness in my chest. The repetition scares me most of all. "I know."

I was going to tell her about my first official date with Robert tonight, but I think I'll wait. She'll appreciate it more when she's having a better day. I'm so excited about tonight I can barely stay in my skin. I wish Rose was feeling better: then everything would be perfect.

She coughs and I'm at her side again. "Are you okay, Rose? You're not getting sick, are you?"

"No, child. I'm fine. Don't make a fuss." She picks up her fork and pushes the grits to one side of her plate but doesn't take a bite.

"Here," I say, "I brought you something." I open the small bag of candied peanuts I know she loves and dump them on her tray. "They're your favorite."

"Indeed they are." She pops a peanut in her mouth.

"You're too good to me, dear."

I'm happy when she starts eating the peanuts with relish and pull another pack from my vest pocket when the first one's gone.

"Knock, knock."

I look up at New York, her ready smile a welcome sight.

"Hey, York."

"How's our girl this morning, huh? You doing okay, Miss Rose?"

"I'm fine," she says without looking up from the peanuts. "I already told Anna not to fuss over me."

New York shrugs and winks at me, her deep-set chocolate eyes laughing. They match her skin, dark and smooth like molasses. She has a tiny frame and arms like twigs, and her pixie-like nose turns up when she notices that Rose hasn't eaten enough to keep a bird alive. But she doesn't say anything about the food because Rose hates being treated like a child. The other nurses say New York's parents got it right when they named her, because she looks like she belongs in the big city rather than small-town Alabama. But looks can be deceiving. She's strong as an ox and loves tending the elderly, and they love her right back.

"So, Anna," New York says, "guess who was fifteen minutes late this morning and forgot his vest?"

I smile wider than I should. "I'm guessing that would be Dustin."

"And you would be correct. He didn't get a full demerit, but if he keeps this up, you'll have no competition for the scholarship at all."

"She doesn't have any competition now," Rose chimes in. "My Anna's getting that scholarship, no question."

"I agree, Miss Rose." New York pats my back. "No one here deserves it more than our girl. Okay, well, I'll be back a little later."

"I'd like to go outside for a while," Rose says when

New York's gone. "Have a little moment in the sun."

"Sure, we can do that," I reply, "but I need to check in on Mr. Nathan first, okay?"

Rose nods and I make my way to the sink, careful to wash every hint of peanuts from my hands. Mr. Nathan's highly allergic, so much so that every red label in this facility that has the words *Allergy Warning* are stuck up in his room somewhere.

"Doesn't a moment in the sun sound heavenly, Anna?"

I hug her before leaving the room and whisper into her good ear. "Yes, Rose. A moment in the sun sounds amazing."

***

Mom stands behind me, making sympathetic clucking noises when I point out that I have nothing to wear that night. "Oh, to be young and beautiful and able to make a garbage bag look good…and still claim to have nothing to wear. Must be nice."

She fiddles with my hair and I let her.

"You ever thought about wearing it up?" She scoops my hair into her hands and plops it on the back of my head. "It would look good up."

"I know how I'm wearing it tonight, but thanks for the suggestion."

I'm wearing it in a braid down my back and pulling a few strands to wisp around my face, because that's how I was wearing it the day I met Robert in the wilderness. Some firsts I *do* remember…

"Well, you should wear a green blouse, to match your eyes."

I appreciate Mom's input, but since it's unseasonably warm, I settle on some high-waisted denim shorts, a blue cami with my flowy white top, and my boots. Maggie always compliments me when I wear white, says it makes me look even darker. And since she cares way more about fashion than me, I figure I should listen to her.

"How 'bout a grilled cheese?"

"I think I'll pass. Robert will be here in about an hour, and we're eating first."

"Well, I have to leave in about forty-five minutes myself, but I hate eating at these things." I expect her to go into the kitchen, but she simply stands in my doorway. I can tell by her fidgeting she wants to ask me something.

"What is it, Mom? Just say it."

The circles under her eyes are so dark that they resemble smudged eyeliner, but I know she's not wearing any makeup. Normally, she'd already be drinking on Saturday afternoon, but she has an office birthday party for her boss in a little while. Thank God she realizes she has to be sober without me having to remind her.

"Well, it's just that you and William were a thing yesterday, and now all of a sudden you decide he's not the one and you already have a date with a guy you met last night. And he's in college. I'm just a little concerned. You can understand that, right?"

I feel a little guilty for not telling her that he's *my* Robert. Okay, so technically I *did* tell her. It's not my fault she was passed out and didn't hear me. But I know her. As upset as she gets over my dreams, she would be so freaked out by this that she'd drink even more just to come to grips with it. No, I can't tell her the truth about me and Robert. Not yet, anyway.

"I do understand, Mom, but you have to trust me. I know what I'm doing, okay? Robert's a super-nice guy, and he's not a complete stranger. I've met him a few times before. Please, no worries."

She sits on my bed again and tugs at a loose string on my comforter. She doesn't look up at me. "You sure you're not just going out with him because his name's Robert, like that guy you dream about?"

My laugh's a little shaky. Her question catches me off guard. "Don't be silly. That's crazy."

This time she stands and looks me dead in the eyes. "Well, maybe so, but I understand crazy."

I let it drop at that and busy myself with my clothing choices.

"I better go find something to wear, too, and fix my face. I really wish I didn't have to go to this thing."

"I'm glad you're going, getting out and socializing. It's a good thing, Mom."

When I look at her again, her face is a pained grimace, and I can tell she's trying not to cry. For a moment I can clearly see both sides of her, the one that's only my mother, the woman who would go to the ends of the earth for me and fight the devil himself to keep me safe. And I can see the other side, the side that's the mother of a dead child and wife of a dead husband. The side that's completely void, completely broken, wanting nothing more than to drink herself into oblivion so she doesn't have to remember her loss, feel the overwhelming agony day in and day out. I just wish she'd realize that her sides will never mesh well together, will never blend, no matter how hard she tries. Calm and chaos have been enemies for way too long.

They will never co-exist.

***

I wait until Mom's out the door to braid my hair. In almost every picture we have of my sister, her hair's braided, so I never wear mine this way. But I want to surprise Robert, see if he reacts to it. And I'll be sure to let it down before Mom sees it. I'm so proud of her for not drinking today. No way I'm doing anything to cause a setback.

My stomach's a complex system of knots and strings, twisting and tingling. I can't remember the last time I've been this nervous and excited all at once. I look at the time on my phone. Robert should be here soon. I remember something else and touch my Facebook app. I open the relationship status on my homepage and remove it altogether, unsure of what the proper etiquette is when you break up with someone. I'm not single, so that would be the wrong choice. And even if I were, switching it to single so quickly after a break-up would seem like a slap in the face to William. I've hurt him enough already. I can't resist looking at his status. He's done nothing with it. It still says he's in a relationship.

I'm startled by the knock on the door but almost run to answer it. When I do, Robert's standing there, the glint in his eyes and the smile I've dreamed of a million times, and I wonder what I ever did in this life to deserve having my dreams come true.

"Hey, you," I say, sounding silly but not really caring. All I care about is being with him.

"Hey." But then he clears his throat. I know the look in his eyes, the look I've seen more clearly than any other in my life, the look that's intended only for me. "Your hair…you wear it like that often?"

"Never."

"Well, you should. You're beautiful."

I say the only three words that pop into my head. "So are you."

He extends a large hand and I take it.

"You ready to go?" he asks.

"I've been ready for a thousand years."

He opens the car door for me and covers his mouth to hide a smile.

"What's so funny?"

"I just realized that I've never opened a car door for you. No cars in our other lives, you know."

He's mindful that I'm completely in before closing the door. And by the button-front shirt he's wearing that resembles almost every shirt he ever owned in the wilderness, I know he's mindful of everything.

We don't say much at first. As excited as I am to be

with Robert, awkward doesn't come close to describing this feeling. To know someone better than you know yourself, but to be separated by time, distance, lives that you've lived together... Overwhelming is an understatement, to say the least. It's unnatural, but as natural as breathing all at the same time. When his hand finds my knee, I relax a little. But I can tell by the trembling that he's nervous, too.

"I'm so glad you remember our last lifetime together," he says, breaking the silence we've been enduring for a couple of minutes now. "I can't tell you how weird it was in our previous lives to know you, but in your eyes I was a total stranger. It was...challenging."

I say what pricks my heart without hesitation. "I can't imagine not knowing you. It feels like I've always known you, Robert. You're the love of my life."

He lifts the back of my hand to his lips and brushes a kiss over it. "And you *are* my life, Anna. Promise me you'll always remember that, no matter what."

"I promise."

***

I'm embarrassed to admit to Robert that I've lived in Tuscaloosa all my life, but I've never been to the Cypress Inn for dinner. Mom and I don't do fancy, and William and I usually just went out to movies or bowling on our dates. And the restaurants were always fast food or pizza.

"So, how was your steak?" Robert asks.

"Amazing. I can't believe I ate the whole thing. I was pretty hungry, though. I skipped lunch because I knew we were eating out tonight."

"Well, I'm glad you enjoyed it. Mine was amazing, too."

The waitress clears our plates and we both decline dessert. Robert points to a dance floor several feet from our table. "You and I have a date there next."

"I think I need to let my food settle for a few minutes

first."

No way I'm admitting that in this lifetime, I have two left feet that probably put all my other lives to shame. I'm surprised he was ever able to teach me to dance. Instead, I ask him a question that's been on my mind since he first mentioned that we've lived several lives together.

"Robert, how did we meet, in our first lifetime, I mean? I want to know what it was like when we *were* strangers—what started all this."

When he's silent, I'm scared I've said something wrong. But after a few seconds, I realize he's drawing clarity, remembering the details so he can fully answer my question.

"I've been so focused on our last lifetime, I haven't given myself the proper time to think about the first. Oh, Canterbury…"

Just hearing him say *Canterbury* that way sends a rush of chills up my arms, and I rub them for relief. It's hard for me to comprehend that we were alive during the Middle Ages.

Robert reaches across the table and takes my hand. "Well, it was 1387 in Canterbury, England. I was nineteen at the time, and a bit of a know-it-all. Your family was well-to-do, and I was convinced, being the artisan I was back then, that I could entice your father to buy these horses I'd carved out of blocks of scrap wood. They were really quite extraordinary."

"My father," I mutter, and Robert grimaces.

"Oh, I'm sorry. That was a little insensitive—"

"No, it's fine," I assure him. "Keep going. Did he like the wooden horses?"

"Well, as it turns out, he was more interested in knowing if I could make a decent longbow for hunting. To my misfortune, he was a practical man who wasn't much into trinkets. So I left defeated that day, but not dissatisfied. On my way off the property, I literally bumped into you, the most beautiful girl I'd ever seen. You were looking down at the needlework you were holding, and I was looking up, muttering about what an imbecile I was for not convincing your father of my worth as an artist. When you opened your mouth to inquire about my well-being, I knew your soul matched your physical appearance. All I thought about after that day was getting to know you better. So I agreed to make that longbow for your father as an excuse to see you. And the rest, as they say, is history. A very long history."

I imagine his words as he speaks, longing to recall it, wishing I could see us in that era as clearly as Robert can. But I can't. I ask instead, "So the woodworking, I guess you've always been a carpenter of sorts, then? In every lifetime?"

"In some capacity, yes."

"I remember the furniture you made, and you built our cabin in the wilderness, too." I smile at the recollection. "And I remember you adding the skylight in our bedroom when I told you that the window was too small and I wished for more sun. No one had ever seen such a creation. You cut out a small part of the roof and added glass to let the light in—"

"But I had to make it so it could be closed when the weather was bad, so I told you we could only use it at certain times. Turns out you wanted it open so much that the ladder I had to use to close it became a permanent fixture on the cabin."

"I have always loved sunlight," I say.

"Well," Robert says, "I have a confession to make."

"And what would that be?"

"You always called it your sunlight catcher, but I enjoyed it more at night. Everything on this earth paled in comparison to you sleeping in our bed, bathed in moonlight when it scattered across the floor. And when that soft light rested on your face…well, let's just say I'd never been more proud of any invention I'd created." He trails a finger along my cheek. "I'd steal moonlight a million times just to see it on your face."

I swallow the lump in my throat. "So, you promised to teach me to dance."

He takes my hand and leads me to the dance floor. The song is slow and gentle, like his hands on my back. We sway and I'm a little clumsy at first, but it doesn't take long to realize why I've never been a good dancer. Up until this very moment, I've been without my partner. His hands and body coax me to follow his motions. And when the music quickens, we're quicker, then slower again and circling.

Robert's breath is in my ear. "See, I told you I would teach you. Do you really not remember dancing when we were in the wilderness?"

"No," I admit again, "but I wish I did."

"It's okay," he says. "I'll show you."

Robert backs away from me, assuming a proper stance and bowing. "Would you do me the honor of this dance, Miss Anna?"

I curtsey because it feels like the right thing to do. "Why certainly, Mr. Grafton."

Every eye in the room is on us now, but I don't care. At this moment, we're the only two people on the planet. Robert guides me to follow his steps, leading me into the motions of an antiquated dance that's smooth and charming, his hand in the small of my back and the other around my extended hand.

"Am I doing this right?" I ask, after I still manage to trip up a little.

"You're doing it perfectly."

When his steps quicken, I stumble forward and he instinctively reaches out to right me again.

"I've got you. Don't worry, I'll never let you fall, Anna."

I bury my face in his chest. "I know. Just hold me."

His hand on my back pulls me closer to him and his other hand cups the back of my head, resting on the braid in my hair. If I hadn't braided it, that hand would be knitting through my loose strands at the moment.

I regret my decision profoundly.

Robert lifts my chin with his knuckle and kisses my nose. "See, I told you I could teach you to dance. So, you ready to get outta here?"

"Show me Canterbury," I say.

"What? Why?"

"Because I'm intrigued. I want to know how we danced for the first time, in Canterbury. Show me."

For several moments, the quiet chatter that once filled the restaurant is reduced to muted voices, even though a few couples have joined us on the dance floor. All I hear are Robert's heavy breaths, his thudding heart, his quickened pulse. He lifts my right arm into the air and coaxes me to turn under our linked appendages. Seconds later I'm at his side, pressing so tightly against it I would believe I'm glued there. I focus on following his lead, afraid I might trip again and make a complete fool of myself. But when his eyes capture mine, I'm dissolved into his memories, can feel his recollections as easily as I feel his hands in mine. We're here now, and nothing else matters. He's no longer wishing for the life he wasn't living. He's complete, and so am I.

"Let's go," I say when the dance is over. "I have a surprise for you."

"Well, now *I'm* intrigued. What is it?"

"It's not a what, it's a where. And I'll show you."

His big, gentle hands make a sandwich around mine, then he tugs my hand to his lips, brushing a small kiss on top. "You can take me anywhere, pretty lady."

We leave the restaurant to a round of applause.

***

Robert looks puzzled when I ask him to turn on my street. "So, we're going back to your place?"

"Not exactly. I mean, it's my place, just not my house."

He pulls over and parks where I tell him to. We step out of the car and I point to the trees.

"That's the *where* I was talking about. I call it The Spot, and you'll love it. It's pretty thick to get through at first, though, so I'll need to lead the way. Oh, and do you have a blanket or something?"

He pulls a towel from the back seat. "Will this do?"

"That's perfect."

I illuminate the flashlight on my phone and hold Robert's hand, tugging him to follow behind me. The night wind slices through the thin air, causing my flowy blouse to blow hard against my face.

"Wow, you weren't joking about this being thick," he says. "Be careful." He holds my hand like we're walking on the edge of glass until we reach the clearing.

"So, what do you think?"

Robert's quiet at first, his head tilted toward the sky. Every star in the heavens is shining down on us, like I ordered this spectacle just for tonight. He finally manages, "This is amazing."

I lay the blanket on the cool grass and we sit.

Robert closes his eyes, like the memory he's sharing is too precious to speak of without some gesture of dignity. "Do you remember how beautiful the night sky was in the wilderness?"

"Not really," I admit. "I wish I *could* recall full details, have the same recollection you do. But like I said before, all my dreams have been scenes, snippets of our lives together. And they all played out in order, right up until the last dream when my throat was slit. I may never dream of our wilderness times again, now that I witnessed my own death." I lay my head on his shoulder. "But I don't need my dreams anymore. I have you."

His large hand trails a line on my throat, and every urge in my body is awakened by his simple touch.

"You know, Anna, being the only one who remembers

our past lives has its demons, too. I wake up in a new life loving you every single day, missing you to the point of insanity, desperate to find you. And when you are found once again, then you love me in the afterglow. I want you to love me completely."

He's never been more wrong. "Make no mistake," I say. "The only way I've ever loved you is completely."

Before I can say another word, his lips cover mine in a kiss that is the reason for the stars to hang so low and shine on us. It's the kind of kiss that creates any brightness that has ever been in the universe. The kiss that has never lost a hint of the intimacy we've shared through countless decades—era after era, time after time. And if I didn't know it before, I know it now with perfect clarity. We are forever bound to each other.

When his lips find my neck, I wince a little.

"Oh, I'm sorry," Robert says. "I forgot about your neck being so sensitive."

"Never apologize for kissing me." I tug his lips to mine again. "Not ever…"

I lay back on the towel when the kissing intensifies, his elbows now nestled on the cool earth near the sides of my face. A soft heat unfurls through me, down my arms, to my stomach, then my legs and toes. I think of nothing and everything all at once. When his lips move from mine to the exposed skin on my chest, I'm not breathing, but more alive than I've ever felt.

"Thank you for loving me," I say, "and for searching for me, for never giving up on me in every lifetime—"

He stops my words with another kiss. "Don't ever thank me for loving you." He cups my face and says just above a whisper, "A single moment I've spent loving you is worth a million moments spent finding you again."

As much as I want to keep kissing him, to lie all night under a blanket of stars, tucked securely in his arms, I have to ask the question that's been running through my head since witnessing my own murder. I sit up and lean close to

Robert's perfect face. "What did you do back then, after I died? I mean, you told me Claude was hanged for my murder, but what happened to you and our babies? I wish I could've watched them grow up. Did you have a lot of trouble raising them without me?"

His breath whooshes out like I kicked him in the gut. A crease of worry dents his brow. "Dammit, I hadn't considered—" But now he's mumbling and I don't understand.

"Hadn't considered what?"

"That you would ask about them…because…*you remember*. Because you loved them—"

The horror I feel obviously shows on my face and stops him mid-sentence. "Robert, what happened to our babies?"

"You have to understand, Anna. When Claude took you from me, he took everything. I hurt to exist without you. I tried, I tried so hard…" His eyes grow bigger and browner, as if that were possible. They bury themselves in mine as he mutters the words. "But I failed them miserably."

I take his hands. "Please, Robert, just tell me what happened."

He draws a couple of shaky breaths. "After I lost you, all I could think about was repeating another life, finding you again. But I couldn't abandon the children. That much I knew. As bad as I hurt, I still did the best I could to take care of them. But I needed something, something to wash away the constant pain. I'm ashamed, Anna, so ashamed… But, I turned to the bottle."

My hands jerk from his. "You started drinking?"

His eyes glass with tears. "Yes."

Images of my mother flash through my spinning brain, and I can't stop the scream that escapes my parted lips. "No! Oh my God, Robert! What did you do?"

"One night after I put the children to bed, I went out to the barn with a bottle of gin. I must've drank the whole thing. I don't know what happened, but that's my last memory of the wilderness."

I gasp. My head's spinning. I can't breathe. "You…you…"

"My next memory is *this* life, Anna. I died in that barn that night."

I'm numb.

I can't feel my arms.

My legs.

My heartbeats.

Nothing.

"How long?" I whisper. "How long after I died did you let this happen?"

"Please, Anna. I didn't mean to—"

"How long!" I scream.

"Two months."

The sobs that tear through me are thunder and rain, a storm I never knew existed. A pain too unbearable to be real. How could he? Not my Robert. How could he allow my babies to be left alone? To suffer? To starve? To die?

"Two months," I say. "You drank yourself to death two months after I died? Our babies could've never survived alone in that cabin. They starved to death," Then it hits me. "It was so cold. Bitterly cold. Oh God. No! They must've frozen to death. Oh God…"

I refuse his offer of comfort when he reaches for me. I doubt I'll ever be comfortable again.

"Anna, please. I'm so sorry. I never meant to die that night. You have to believe me. That was never supposed to happen—"

"I have to go." It's all I can manage.

I leave him standing in the clearing and head for the trail. I don't bother with the light. I run. Just run—can never run fast enough to make his words go away. My babies. My sweet babies. The sheer, white top I'm wearing over my cami catches on a branch, and I allow it to be ripped from my body. What's the difference? My heart's been ripped out, too. No way I'm slowing down.

Within minutes I'm in my driveway and headed for the front door. I hear the blaring music and my stomach clenches. No way. Not this time. Mom's words are slurred, mixed with guttural sounds I can't make out, but I don't care. I don't want to hear her drunken words, her worthless chatter.

I lean close to her ear and push through gritting teeth. "You're filthy, stinking drunk. Again!"

"You can't...speak to me...like that," she says, never lifting her head off the sweat-soaked couch.

"Then how about I stop speaking to you altogether, huh? If you need me, don't even utter my name!"

I bolt into my bedroom and slam the door. I cry out, memories of my cherished babies flooding my reeling brain. Then I imagine Robert, drunk and dying. I fall to my knees. I'm thinking. Overthinking. Suffocating—having my throat slit all over again, but it's much worse now. I see Robert Jr.'s tiny face again, but this time he's blue, ice cold, wondering why his mommy has abandoned him, left him to die in a frozen wilderness. My chest aches when Emily's image rushes through me, my precious infant, so wee and innocent. I scream, but no one hears me. I just keep screaming...

CHAPTER 11

The last several days are a blur. Robert's been blowing up my phone, but I don't care. Twice I almost answered just to hear his voice, to see if his pain matches mine even in the slightest. But he's had longer to process this—much longer knowing the fate of our babies. Well, I need time to process, time to forgive him…if that's even possible.

Maggie's lips are an unstoppable force of nature. I wonder if they ache from the constant movement. She's prattling on about everything and nothing. It's amazing, but she's even managed to drown out the cafeteria noise, or maybe my own tired brain's doing that. Either way, it's fine with me.

The universe is a twisted sister. I guess she thought it was funny, giving me a dead father and sister in this life, and a mother who drinks herself into oblivion in order to numb the pain of losing them. Is that supposed to give me some kind of ingrained understanding, some deep, instilled empathy for Robert's selfishness? Hell, I know he didn't do it on purpose and would go back and change it a million times over if he could. No one ever has to prove to me how much he loved our children. Well, my mom loves me too, and doesn't hurt me on purpose, either. But that doesn't make the consequences of her selfishness any less painful or real. Sooner or later, something ends up broken. I'm just tired of that something being me.

Maggie pokes my arm when I'm a gazillion miles away instead of listening to her.

"Did you even hear me? I'm in the middle of a crisis," she says. "God, you've been acting so bizarre."

"I'm sorry," I say. "Tell me again. I'm listening now, I swear."

She huffs for dramatic effect. "Like I said, Kyle asked me to go to the movies with him Friday night, but Eden promised that if I met up with her at the football game, she'd introduce me to her cousin, Daniel. He's so hot, but Kyle's pretty major, too. What should I do?"

This is what she considers a crisis? God, I would kill to have her problems.

"I don't know, Mags. I mean, at least Kyle goes to school here. Where does this Daniel person even live, if Eden's hooking you two up?"

"Duh. He lives here, but he goes to Central, like William." Her face gets all animated. "Hey, he's a senior, too. Maybe he already knows Will. That would be cool, right? We could double and it wouldn't be awkward at all."

"It would be way awkward," I say. "I broke up with William almost a week ago."

She drops her fork. "Shut up! Why didn't you tell me?"

Now I huff at her, but for an entirely different reason. "Because it's not that big of a deal. He wanted to get way too serious way too fast, and I didn't. End of story."

She flips a blond curl from her shoulder and brushes a piece of lint off her sleeve. "Wow. Didn't see that coming. Well, that makes my decision a little easier, then. Let me catch Kyle before lunch wave's over. See ya in fourth block, okay?"

I nod my approval then pick up the untouched apple from my tray. I go to take a bite but stop before it reaches my mouth as I'm struck by the memory of a wilderness dream I had last year. It was Christmas Eve, and Robert had surprised me with several jars of apple preserves. He'd bartered for them from an elderly woman he'd made a table for. I was pregnant with Robert, Jr. at the time, and those apples were equivalent to gold or silver to me. And Robert knew it. It was thoughtful, appreciated—the perfect gift. The perfect… But then I see my babies' sweet smiles and stop the reminiscing. I drop the apple on my tray and pull out my Calculus book to cram for a test we have in the morning.

My phone sounds a text alert. Oh God. It's William.

Hope you're okay.
Hope we can still
be friends. If not ☹

I'm relieved he sounds better, not so angry, but I'm nowhere near ready to hang out with him or anything. I text back a simple smiley face and wish him well. And I *do* wish him well. But I mainly just wish he'd forget about me. He's too sweet to be hurt from any of this. Why does he have to be so sweet?

***

It shouldn't feel so foreign, his breath on my face and his soft warmth in my ear as he whispers, "I love you, Anna. I've always loved you…"

My eyes pop open when the clock on the living room wall chimes four. I don't remember falling asleep on the couch after school, but my nights have consisted of mostly tossing and turning since learning the fate of my babies, so it's not too surprising. I touch my cheek, remembering Robert's words from the dream—my normal dream, not a flashback. I smile at the irony. As hurt and angry as I am, I can't deny the fact that I miss him, and I'm glad my mind's allowed him back into my subconscious. Now I have to find a way to let go of the pain that's consuming me and let him back in completely.

Part of me knows it's fruitless, anyway. My children died many years ago. There was never a possibility for them to be alive in the here and now. Of course I know that—have always known that fact. But every hope and dream I ever had for them consisted of my tiny prodigies growing up, getting married, having families, growing old. And in my memories—my aspirations for their lives— their last breaths were taken knowing that they'd lived fully, happily. The imagined paths I'd laid out for them always brought me pure joy. But now, even my real memories of them—of Robert, Jr. playing with his ball on the porch, or my sweet Emily swaddled tightly against my chest—bring me nothing but pain, knowing that after I left them in the wilderness, precious little time was given to them on this earth. Well, I can't accept it. How can I ever accept it? Does Robert even realize that when he drank himself to death, he stole our future? He left us all in that wilderness.

Mom won't be home from work for another hour or so. I'm starving, but it's Wednesday. She usually gets us a sack of cheeseburgers off the dollar menu from McDonald's on Wednesdays because it's payday. She always jokes about how easy to please we are…how a cheat day is the highlight of our week and she loves our simple, down-to-earth tastes. Well, the cheeseburgers are great, but I'll never admit to her the real reason I look forward to Wednesdays. Wednesday is the one day of the week I can depend on Mom to take care of me for a change, even if it is with fast food.

When my stomach starts gnawing into my backbone, I give in and grab a bag of chips from the pantry. I settle back on the couch with my Calculus book and the chips when my phone makes a text alert. It's Robert.

Please don't shut me out.

We need to talk. Will you
come over? I'm so
sorry, Anna. Please...

As much as I want to stay angry with him, deep down I know it's time to talk. The more I consider it, the more I realize how much easier it would have been for him to simply lie to me about the fate of our children. But he didn't. He told me the truth without hesitation, and I know that was beyond difficult for him. So it's time. I need to hear what he has to say. I reply with three words.

Be there soon.

***

Robert's standing outside his apartment door as I pull into the parking lot. It's like he's been waiting there for me since I left him at The Spot several nights ago, like he hasn't moved, hasn't taken a breath. His arms are outstretched, and I walk into his awaiting hug.

"I'm so sorry, Anna," he says. "You'll never know how much I regret that night in the barn. And I've never drank as much as a drop of alcohol in this lifetime, I swear it."

"I believe you," I say, inhaling his scent, a mixture of earth and mint, and releasing some of the hurt that's been building over the last several days. "I believe you."

I can tell in his voice that he's holding back tears. "You know, the other night, that was the first time you've ever left me willingly. Death has ripped you from me, but you've never walked away from me by choice. Anna, please don't ever *choose* to leave me. I could never bear it. Never."

I look in his eyes. And not just a glance, but I bore into them, like he needs to hear me now more than any other time in our entire existence. "Robert, I'm not leaving you, but I need to know why. I need to know more. You know

111

everything, but up until now I've known very little or nothing at all about our *situation*. You've been traveling the road home for centuries, but I've been on different roads, different levels of understanding. There has to be a reason why this is happening to us, why we're repeating. And I deserve to know the truth, right here, right now. Do you understand?"

He nods and leads me into the apartment. We sit on the couch and he takes a deep breath.

"When you died in the wilderness," he says, "I knew I wouldn't see you again until our next lifetime. And you have to understand, Anna, our other lives were never like this. In all the others, you've never known me in the slightest. I've always had to meet you all over again, I had to make you fall in love with me all over again and then convince you that we've shared other lives together. You will never know how difficult it was for me, to love you so purely and completely, and for you not to know me at all.

"But when you died in the wilderness, it was even worse. Then we had children. How would I ever help you remember them in the next life when you never remembered me? So, I came up with a plan. I took the silver rattle that had belonged to both of them and buried it under a large rock next to the river where we met. I hoped that one day you would see it, hold it in your hands, and maybe it would help you to remember them. After all, I was going to have the pleasure of raising them, so in the next life I wanted you to have something." He cups my cheek. "Do you remember the silver rattle?"

I can't speak at first, can't move. Hot tears land on my face and I manage to squeak out, "Yes, I remember the rattle."

"Good." He reaches into a small drawer in the end table next to him and places the rattle inside my shaking hands. "No item in this world has been more important than this rattle to me since the day I retrieved it. It is the only thing I have left of them, of our children. It is precious to me, and now it's yours. Nothing in this world is more precious to me then you, Anna."

I turn the rattle around and around in my fingers, rubbing the weathered silver, wanting to feel every groove, every ridge. I'm so overwhelmed, I'm speechless. My babies touched this, held this, listened to me shake it in front of their tiny faces and smiled at the soft, tinkling noise it created, time and time again. I shake it and cry out when the faint sound lifts into the air.

"Oh God," I say. "But…how?"

"Right after I moved here, I found our river on the internet. You'll never know how happy I was to see that huge rock I'd buried it under, right there on Google Earth. So I used some of the money I'd saved and flew to Michigan. It wasn't easy, but I dug it up."

I hold the rattle against my chest, sobs tearing through me in waves. I'd never considered holding something so precious, something that belonged to my babies. I'm whole and shattered all at once. I can't believe Robert did this for me, for us.

He kneels in front of me and hugs my knees, his face on my lap. "You have to understand, I never intended to die in the barn that night. I'd never been a drinker, so I didn't realize it *could* kill me. I know it sounds pathetic, but it's true."

I stroke his cheek and say through my tightened throat, "I believe you, and I'm trying in every way to understand. You've had longer to process it, though."

He looks up, his jaw clenched. "I've had longer to feel guilty, you mean. I feel guilty every day of my life. You have to know that."

I'm quiet, holding tightly to the rattle and resting in the comfort it's generating. Robert stands, then sits on the couch with me again, covering my hands and the rattle with his.

"You know," he says, "after I lost you, I came really close to destroying the music box I made you—"

"Oh, you didn't!"

"No," he assures, "I didn't. At first I hated it, though. Every time I looked at it, I remembered you offering it to Claude, thinking it would save me. You were so brave. Well, one night when I was missing you desperately and on the verge of insanity from grief, I picked it up and held it over my head. I had every intention of smashing it into a million pieces. But then I remembered your face the day I gave it to you. When excitement lights your eyes, you shame the sun, you know that? So, I couldn't do it. But I did modify it, in a way."

I sit up straighter. "Modified it? How?"

"Well, I remember you playing it for Emily one afternoon and promising our daughter that one day it would be hers. So, I carved inside the lid *This box belonged to Anna Grafton. Pass it to her only daughter, Emily, and all who follow in her line.*"

I squeeze my eyes closed, picturing Emily's sweet face, wishing I remembered the day he's recalling, but I don't. But I do know one thing—Robert truly believed Emily would own my music box one day. He wanted our children to have a future.

"How do you do it?" I ask. "How do you ever get over what we lost in that lifetime?"

He takes me in his arms, his kisses starting at the crease of my neck, and slowly trailing to my chin. His soft nibbles tickle my skin, but I don't dare move. He grasps my face in his powerful hands and kisses me so deeply that I'm stealing his breaths just to exist. We're one being, one soul, like the universe has forever intended. And when the kiss is over, I'm merely half myself again.

He whispers into my hair, "The first time I kissed you, my world as I knew it was gone, and there was only you. So you see, my love, it's not about knowing what I've lost in those lifetimes. It's about knowing what I have to lose, right here, right now. I've suffered many losses, Anna…and not just in the wilderness."

My eyes widen, his words like electric shocks pulsing through my chest. "What do you mean?"

"It's time you knew the truth. You deserve to know everything."

CHAPTER 12

We both sit there, surrounded in a silence that should be awkward, but it affords me time to soak it in. This is it. The end—the end of everything I ever thought was true about my past-life dreams, my other life with Robert. For so long, my dreams held comfort, escape, were a safe haven to fall into when everything else in my life was way too hard most of the time. Deep down, I've always known that's why I never tried to research anything about Robert, even when I was sure that what was happening to me had everything to do with real memories and nothing at all to do with elaborate fantasies or random streams of consciousness, like most therapists would have one believe. But I'm ready for the truth now. I need it more than anything. I'm just glad he's willing to give it to me.

Robert clears his throat and I hold my breath.

"Some of this is going to be tough to hear," he says.

"I understand." I clutch the silver rattle tighter.

He smiles, but it doesn't hide the tears threatening his eyes. "Wanna know something funny? Most men believe they are the masters of their fates, but that couldn't be further from the truth. Fate is the master, and we are the souls it controls. Sometimes we seek out the ghosts and do everything in our power to drive them away. But sometimes the ghosts seek us. And you can be assured of one thing. When the ghosts do the seeking, they always win."

"I don't understand—"

"In every lifetime, before we meet, you belong to another." He drags his hands through his hair so tightly it causes him to squint. "You belong to another, but you fall for me, and it's as natural as breathing, like no one else in the world exists but us." He takes my hands as if he has to hold them to keep me from slipping away. "But if you don't take anything else from the things I'm about to tell you, promise me you'll believe that you've always been mine. No other man has ever truly claimed your heart. That gift has always been mine and mine alone."

The words show in his eyes, which are rounder and darker, with yellow flecks running through them that I hadn't noticed until this moment.

"No one ever has to convince me of that, Robert. You own my heart."

He blinks away the shine of tears and I freeze, too afraid to say another word. Robert has always been massive and strong, like a hundred-year-old oak—firm, sure, grounded. But now he seems as fragile as a twig. I'm careful not to respond badly, too afraid I might snap him in two.

His mouth is a tight line. "But I lose you, Anna, in every lifetime. Death finds you when you're very young, and I lose you…over and over again."

The words turn to fire in my veins, smoldering in my body like embers atop gray ash. They ignite my flesh, poison my blood with heat until my soul is screaming to rationalize every piece of what he's saying to me.

I die.

Young.

Every time.

"But when I saw Claude kill me, I asked if you were

here because I'm going to die. Is Claude repeating too? Am I in danger—?"

"Just listen to me, Anna. Claude's been dead and buried for two hundred years, and he's not coming back. He's not *the somebody* who's important in any of this…"

"Then who is?"

"The man who led him to our cabin that day."

I'm confused at first, but then the flashback of that day hits me. I remember seeing Robert talking to a couple of men on horseback. I remember the words *You should have never brought him here…*

"Who was he?" I ask. "Who brought Claude to our cabin that day?"

He touches my face and attempts a smile. "I thought it would be obvious." He pulls me closer to him and I settle in, bracing myself for the words that will follow.

"He was the young man who was courting you before we met," Robert says. "That's always how I lose you. I'm the cause of another young man getting his heart broken, and then he ultimately shatters mine."

It's hard to speak, hard to know what questions to ask first. I just want him to tell me everything…everything I don't remember, everything I need to know. So I say the only five words running through my head. "Just start from the beginning."

His voice is a little reedy, so he clears it. "Canterbury, 1387, was our beginning. That was the first year we met. I loved you from the start, from that first day I bumped into you after leaving your father's study. He'd commissioned me to make a longbow for him. Remember that story?"

"I do."

"Well, your father was more than pleased with the bow, and he had me make more for his hunting companions. He was so pleased that ultimately he didn't refuse when I asked to court you. But when you and I first met, you had been dating a young man who worked the cattle for your father—"

"What was his name?" I say. I'm not sure why it matters, why I feel I need to know.

Robert's cheeks flush a burning red, and I'm immediately sorry for asking. "Adam," he says, "and I'm not sure what you saw in him in the first place. He always smelled of cow dung and sweat, and his face was usually creased with dirt."

I snuggle closer against his side and he continues.

"Anyway, you and I were wed on June 28, 1388, and Adam continued to work for your father. After we're married for a year…"

Robert pauses and takes my hand, as though the words are almost unbearable to say.

"After we're married a year," he says, "you're in an accident involving Adam, and I lose you. I never even got the chance to say goodbye. You were only nineteen."

"What happened?" My throat's so dry it sounds more like a croak than a question.

"Adam and another young man were working in the hayloft in your father's cattle barn. I had been helping out that day, too, because one of the other workers had fallen ill. You thought I was working in the loft, and you'd brought plum cakes for each of us. But I was in the adjoining barn, checking in on a pregnant mare. Somehow, Adam lost his footing and started to fall from the loft. When you tried to help him, you both fell. It wasn't a very high fall. Adam only suffered a broken shoulder…" His eyes glass and his voice sounds phlegmy. "I was on my way back to the hayloft when I heard you scream. I watched you hit the ground, but there wasn't a damn thing I could do. You landed headfirst…broke your neck. You were dead before I could make it to your side."

"Oh God, Robert. That's horrible. I'm so sorry." All I want to do is comfort him, console him and promise that I'll never leave him again. Then it hits me. "But you were so young when I died. And that was our first lifetime together. You had no way of knowing we'd be repeaters.

Why didn't you ever remarry?"

He looks at me like the thought makes him ill. "I don't know, but I just couldn't. Once you have a love that's so true and complete, how could anyone ever measure up, ever fill that void? And honestly, it would have been unfair for me to expect it from another. So I locked your memory away like treasure. Your memories were all I had left, and I made them enough."

He cups my face and kisses me so tenderly that I freeze, wanting to feel every drop of warmth, every eyelash touch of breath and flesh.

He whispers, "Every memory of you has always been enough for me."

As badly as I want to do nothing but comfort him, I need to know more, need to know what happened in the sixteenth century. "I'm so sorry you endured so much loss, Robert, but I need to know the rest, okay?"

His face becomes determined, focused, as if he's about to give a speech he's rehearsed a hundred times. He's pushing down the pain now. Whatever he's about to tell me can't be good. Has to be much worse than Canterbury.

"I was born in my second life in 1562, and I don't ever know of a time that I didn't remember our lives together in Canterbury. I suppose by the time I reached the age of understanding, I knew that I was repeating. And the love I carried for you was as strong as the first day I met you in our previous life. I prayed to our Maker that somehow you were repeating, too."

I'm glued to his words, hurting that he's been burdened with such a curse...the curse of loving me.

"In that life in London," he continues, "I was an intern for a famous artisan furniture maker. Your father hired my boss to redecorate the dining hall in your home. When we arrived, your father was introduced to me as Master Berkeley, and I nearly collapsed—"

"From hearing his name? I'm sure he wasn't the only Berkeley—"

"No, not from hearing his name. From glancing over his shoulder and seeing a family painting hanging on the wall, with you in it. His precious daughter, Anna. I had to feign an ailing stomach just to step outside and compose myself. But I was the happiest man on the planet that day, on the day I had found you once again."

I'm hanging on his words, loving the lift in his voice and the shine of his eyes when he speaks of me.

"Needless to say, your father's furniture order became my priority. My boss was so happy with my work and attention to detail that I was sent to personally deliver a table design to see if it met with your mother's approval. Your mother was so pleased with my design that she called you into the room, and my world started spinning again. You walked in that dining hall, and it took every ounce of strength I could muster to keep from taking you in my arms and smothering you with kisses."

"How did you hold it together?" I ask.

"It wasn't easy, I can assure you. But after a few seconds, I simply smiled and introduced myself. You see, my love, it was obvious that I was a stranger to you. We were both repeating, but I was the only one who knew it."

Suddenly I feel guilty, sorry that I wasn't exactly like Robert—sorry that I hadn't been waiting for him, searching for him, loving him in every lifetime. He's right about the demons. His are unequivocally more torturous than mine.

"So what did you do?" I know how obvious the answer is, but need to hear his explanation just the same.

Robert tugs me closer to his side and whispers in my hair. "I hoped and prayed you'd fall in love with me again, but in London it was quite *difficult*."

"Because you remembered and I didn't?" It's more a statement than a question.

"No, because you were betrothed, and I wasn't."

Betrothed? That possibility never entered my thoughts. Oh God, my poor Robert. I want to cry out, but I'm quiet, listening instead to his recollection and hating the emotional roller coaster he's ridden through hundreds of years.

"As it would be," Robert continues, "your father had arranged your marriage only two years prior, but you had little feeling for the young man. In fact, you barely knew him. You were your mother's only daughter, and she loved you beyond measure. When she became aware of your feelings for me, she convinced your father to break your engagement. And I was a pretty good catch, in my own right. I was a master craftsman, after all."

I put a shaky hand on my stomach to calm the nerves that have been gnawing a hole through me since Robert started recounting our past lives. "Okay, well, that doesn't seem too bad," I say. "If my mother was in agreement with us being together, then it had to be a clean break from the other dude, right?"

Robert's quiet for several seconds, his mouth merely a line again. "I wish it were that simple," he says, "but I learned a long time ago that things rarely are." His gaze connects with mine. "He didn't like losing, and even after you and I were married, he found ways to come around. We lived on your parents' estate, in what was originally a guest house, but it stayed unoccupied most of the time. You loved that house, Anna. You made it ours in no time. And we were so happy.

"But one night, after we'd been married for six months, your old suitor showed up at our door in the middle of the night. He kept saying that you were supposed to be his, that I had stolen you away from him. I tried to reason with him, tried to make him understand, but he wouldn't listen. I was unarmed, but he was holding two swords."

I gasp, my eyes filling with hot tears. "Oh God…"

"He challenged me to a duel."

I'm not moving. Not breathing. I'm listening, focusing, trying to imagine what we were going through, why every lifetime we've had so far seems to end so badly.

"There was no way I could refuse him, either." Robert's eyes are now glass, and I can see his soul as he speaks. "We were in grave jeopardy, Anna. Everything happened so quickly. He tossed the sword to me and lunged. I had to fight him, defend myself and you. I fought with everything I had, but eventually he overpowered me. But instead of running me through right then and there, he started taunting me. And you, being my sweet, pure Anna, you tried to defend me. You jumped in front of me when you saw the sword about to come down. He even tried to pull the sword back when he realized you were falling into it. But it was too late…much too late…"

His voice cracks and I search his face.

"He drove that sword almost clean through you and I lost you…both."

"Both?"

His large hand covers mine and the silver rattle I'm still clutching. "You were pregnant with our first child, Anna. His sword took you both from me that night."

I can't stop the sobs that shred me. "Why?" I scream over and over. "Why is this happening to us?" I'm shaking so hard it feels like shivers from cold, so I wrap my arms around Robert's middle. "Please tell me why this is happening."

"I honestly don't know," he says, hugging me so tightly that it almost hurts. "But the one thing I do know is that I love you with everything I have, and I've done everything in my power to keep you safe…in every lifetime. But it seems that the only promise I have ever made to you that I haven't broken is a love that is never going to end. Love's supposed to be enough." He kisses my forehead and says against my skin, "Why can't it ever be enough?"

His sincere words remind me of what we've already been through, what we've faced together century after century, time after time. And yet, here we are still, bound to each other with nothing but a promise of love. As scared as I am of the unknown, of what we might have to face in this life, of one fact I'm certain: even a hint of love with Robert is enough to keep me at his side forever.

"I want to be a better man," he says. "I try so hard in each new life, wondering what I did wrong in the previous ones, trying to avoid the same mistakes…"

"Shhh." I find his lips and kiss him hard, hard enough to pull him from his demons, hard enough that he's only focused on me, on the present, on what we may have both done right this time. When I have his full attention, I tug my lips from his, my breath catching when I actually consider the here and now. "I broke William's heart, too, you know, but it almost sounds too ridiculous to consider he would be like the others. There's just no way. We'd only been dating a couple of months. I mean, we never even…"

Robert trails a finger across my arm and my stomach tingles. "Never what?" he asks.

Sitting here beside him, touching his skin and looking into his eyes so deeply I could fall into them, it seems impossible—impossible to handle any of this. How do I accept the loss he's described, endure the pain the universe has dealt us? I want to believe so badly that our past lives have nothing to do with the present. After all, this is a different generation, more modern times. I'm not promised to another man. I'm free to make my own choices. But there is one truth I know, a part of me I've held on to so dearly that it actually amazes me how casually most people give it up. But maybe it has something to do with this vicious cycle. Maybe it's the one difficult choice that makes a difference somehow.

"I never did *anything* with William," I say. "I'm…I'm a virgin."

He watches me carefully, then says matter-of-factly. "I know."

He knows. I feel so exposed I cross my arms in front of my chest just to keep the rest of my heart from pouring out. "You know?"

"Well, I was hoping. Things are so different in this

century, but deep down I knew you would be. Hey, wanna know a secret? I've never even kissed another girl, not since I met you."

My face turns in his direction like a cannon blast exploded. He can't be serious. I knew he said he'd never been with another girl after me, but not even a kiss?

"You've never kissed another girl—"

"Not since I met you over six hundred years ago." He lifts my chin with his knuckle. "Hey, what can I say? You made quite the impact."

His lips find mine and he tastes like ocean and nectar, like green fields and fresh air and everything worth traveling spans of roads and millions of miles just to take it all in, to be a part of something bigger than myself. I weave my fingers through his hair, urging him deeper into my mouth, hoping somehow he'll devour all the uncertainty in our future and blot out any danger that lies ahead.

"Anna," Robert says when the kiss is over, "I do truly believe we're free now, in this life. Think about it. This is the only time you've ever remembered anything about our history together. You remember the wilderness, you knew me when I walked up to you in that mall. And, forgive me for being so blunt, but you love me."

"With all my heart."

"And because you fall in love with me, again and again in every lifetime, then that has to be a good omen, a sign that we're meant to be together. I just have to find the puzzle piece that's missing that will allow us to live happily ever after."

He pulls my hand to his lips and kisses it so tenderly that my knees feel wobbly. "But I do think William is harmless, too. Like you said, you'd only been dating him for a short time—"

"And he's a nice guy," I add.

Robert smiles. "My sweet, compassionate Anna." He seems to take his first real breath since our conversation began. "I certainly hope so. Just be mindful of him, though. We kind of have a bad history."

"Well, you do know the best way to handle history, don't you?"

He looks confused.

I lean close to his ear and whisper, "Rewrite it."

"You know what? I think maybe we already have."

His mouth covers mine as if I'm breath and sky, like I'm freedom and immortality instead of the poison death our love always seems to create for us. But if we are truly poison, toxic instead of safe, death instead of the everlasting life that repeating seems to offer, then I will allow his kisses to be my drug and believe with every piece of my soul that his kiss alone will save me.

CHAPTER 13

It's hard when I'm home again, so very hard to leave him when I know he's been without me for way too long. I think about Mom's drinking, about the struggle she's faced losing my dad and sister. For as many times that I've tried to convince her that she has to move on, has to realize that there's a life here without them, my heart breaks in a million pieces imagining how Robert has managed to survive after watching me die over and over again. He's the most courageous person I've ever known and could be an inspiration to my mother. I need to find a way to tell her he's here. She needs to look bravery in the eyes and steal a little of it for herself.

I open the fridge in search of the cheeseburgers, but there aren't any. I grab a granola bar instead, eat it in a few bites, and then chase it down with a can of diet soda. No cheeseburgers on our junk food night can only mean one thing—she's drinking during the week now. *And things will be a gazillion times harder...*

She's sleeping when I check in on her. I watch the slow rise and fall of her chest for a few seconds and remove the photo of my dad from her hand before turning off her bedroom light. I make my way to my own room, my head still spinning from the revelations Robert shared with me. Could it be possible that I'm going to die young in this lifetime, too? My God, what would that do to my mother? But I already know the answer to that question: it would end her, push her so far into oblivion that, without me here to pull her out, it would completely suck her away. But I push the thoughts from my tired mind. That's not going to happen this time. We're not in the dark ages anymore, and Will and I weren't betrothed or super-serious or anything. Maybe this twisted universe is finally rewarding Robert for his suffering...rewarding him with *me*. I smile at the notion and get ready for bed.

***

New York's coaching a couple of freshman girls who just signed up to be Sunshine Warriors. One of the other elder care nurses had to go home early because her child's sick. That means every nurse here is making rounds, which leaves me in charge of counting the supplies that were just unloaded from the stock truck an hour ago. But it's okay. I've never minded taking inventory.

I count the cartons of gloves, face masks, and antibacterial soaps and write the numbers in the appropriate blocks on my clipboard. Then I count the gauze, syringes, and wound care items and log them in, too. New York will have to enter the numbers in the computer later, though. They don't allow volunteers to touch the computers.

After everything's counted, I load the items on a large handcart and head to the supply closet. Rose's room is only three doors away, and she's my next stop when I finish stocking. I can't wait to tell her what Robert's revealed to me over the last several days, although I do plan to sugarcoat some of it. I never want her to fear for my safety, and telling her I've died young in *every* lifetime would freak her out way too much. And I've been really worried about her lately. I hope she's having a better day.

I push the handcart into the hallway after I'm finished in the closet and stop at Rose's door when I hear voices. I recognize the male one immediately.

Robert.

I've mentioned to Robert a couple of times that I wanted him to meet Rose. I can't believe he showed up here on his own to do just that, without any urging from me. The reasons why I love him keep stacking up like sandbags in a flood. I tuck a stray hair behind my ear and check the front of my uniform before entering the room. Robert and Rose are seated side by side in front of her window, people-watching.

"Well, hello dear," Rose says when she sees me. "I told your young man here you'd be along soon."

"I hope you don't mind, Anna," Robert says, "but I knew you were working this morning and I really wanted to meet Rose and see what you do around here. They told me you were stocking and I didn't want to interrupt, so I decided to just introduce myself to Rose and visit with her for a little while—"

"Introduce?" Rose says. "There was no need for introductions. I recognized Robert immediately from all the times you've told me about your wilderness dreams, Anna, and he's every bit as handsome as you've described."

Robert cracks a half-smile, and a flush of pink heat rushes up my cheeks.

I whisper close to his ear. "You know you just made her entire week, right? And mine, too. You're amazing."

"Me? Amazing? Nope." He winks. "Rose here is the one who's amazing. Do you know how nice it is to finally meet someone who totally gets that we've lived other lives together, without looking at me like I'm a total crazy person? And when she said my name before I had the chance to introduce myself, I have to admit...it was awesome."

Rose chuckles. "Well, since my father never owned oil wells or diamond mines, and I was never an heiress in disguise, and since my husband never fended off hungry alligators or crossed the Sahara just to seek my hand in marriage, let's just say that Anna's recollections of her past life with you have brought more excitement and romance to my life than I've ever known. She's a treasure."

Robert lifts Rose's hand and places a small kiss on top. "A classic beauty like you not having much romance in your life? Now that I find hard to believe."

I can see a bit of lipstick on Robert's cheek, the obvious evidence of an earlier kiss from Rose, but I don't dare tell him to rub it away. It's the sweetest thing I've seen in this room for weeks, and the brightest I've seen Rose's smile in days. I'll happily allow him to display it.

"Well, my boy," Rose says, "there was plenty of love in my life, don't get me wrong. My Ted was everything to me, and I loved him with all that I had. Problem is, I'm not sure I ever really told him just how much I loved him. When love is safe, you tend to keep it that way—safely tucked away in your heart, believing that with each passing day your partner will simply know you love them because you're still there. But my Ted deserved to hear it more, to hear it better."

Robert and I are quiet, lost in her words like paper boats adrift on a forever sea.

"Yes, our love was safe, humdrum, and comfortable. It never faced the challenges you and Anna have endured."

She's quiet and faraway for several seconds, so I add, "I guess Robert and I are part of a timeless love story."

"No," Rose corrects, "you *are* the timeless love story."

For the next hour we talk about everything and nothing—about Rose's childhood and her favorite horse who took every opportunity to sit in a mud puddle when he spotted one, regardless of whether or not she was still on his back, to which Jell-O tastes best in the cafeteria, the red or the green.

When my shift's almost over, I squeeze Robert's hand and say to Rose, "Time for me to get outta here for the day. You need anything before we leave?"

"You've given me so much already, sweet girl. I'm fine. Go. You're young. Enjoy the rest of your Saturday."

When Robert offers her a hug, she tugs him closer to her face. "I always believed you were real, you know. I never doubted a single dream Anna ever shared with me about your life in the wilderness. I'm glad you found her again. That was the pleasant surprise neither one of us ever considered or expected. But life is full of those, dear boy— surprises. Don't ever forget that."

Rose's eyes are glassier than I've noticed lately, and she coughs before she speaks again.

"She deserves you, Robert. You deserve each other. Promise me you'll always take care of her."

He covers her hands with his. "I promise."

***

"It's fairly recent, but I'm worried," I admit when Robert asks me how long Rose has had her cough. "She always says it's no big deal, but she's been looking really tired lately."

"I'm sure she's fine," he says. "And she seemed so happy today. I'm glad I got to meet her. She's awesome."

"She really is, and don't tell Maggie, but Rose is my best friend in the world. I don't know how I would've made it through the last couple of years without her."

Robert nods then picks up another slice of pizza. It was his idea to walk across the street for lunch after we left the nursing home. The weather's so nice that we decided to eat outside. Even though it's fall, it feels more like spring.

"You know, I'm not sure how we survived our other lifetimes without pizza. Am I right?" He pulls a gooey string of cheese off his finger and plunks it into his mouth.

"Well, the meat pies I used to make in the wilderness

sort of resembled pizza—"

He shakes his head. "Uhhh…nope."

I can't stifle the laugh. "Not even a little bit?"

"Anna, I love you, but no."

There they are again, the three words that come as natural as breathing for him, and have probably been spoken between us thousands of times in our pasts, yet in this life, they're raw and new. My heart speeds each time he professes it, and I want nothing more than to give him all the love he deserves. And I *do* love Robert, with all I have. But part of me wonders if I'm worth everything he's been through just to be with me.

"Why does it always end so badly for us?" I say.

He drops the pizza and takes my hand. "Whoa, where'd that come from?"

"Nowhere, really. I was just thinking about everything you've told me, about how I've died young in every lifetime. Why does that keep happening? What's wrong with us? Why does every future we have together end so badly?"

"I don't know," he says, "but I am sure of one thing."

"Oh, yeah. What's that?"

"There is no future for me without you."

I nod. We don't need words right now. I know exactly what he means. No matter how my racing brain gets the better of me at times, I know without a doubt that I would meet a hundred deaths for that one single lifetime when we just might get it right.

When I start eating again, another question mingles with the pizza—finds its way into my mouth and through my lips before I can stop it. "Are you afraid of dying? I mean, I'm the one who dies before you every time, right?"

Robert's jaw tightens. "Yes, that's right."

"Well, then I'll ask again. Are you afraid to die?"

"No."

"Then what are you afraid of?"

"Living without you."

I swallow the tears that threaten to fall. "Oh." It's all I can say.

Robert cups my chin, stroking my cheek with his thumb. "Listen to me, Anna. I know you've had a lot to deal with over the last few days. Part of me was scared to death you'd take off the second I told you about your untimely deaths, but I promise you this. I'm not the same man I was in those days, in those lives. I've learned and I've sacrificed. I've atoned for the mistakes I've made, and as long as there is breath in me, I will keep you safe. I swear it, Anna." He lightly squeezes my chin. "And when this life is through, I will see wrinkles on that gorgeous face of yours."

"You want me to have wrinkles?"

"I've never watched you grow old."

"And you want to see me old?"

"Every day of my life."

I close my eyes, savoring his response. His simple confession comforts me more than I thought possible. I believe in my bones that he desires to grow old with me, and I believe in my soul he would crush mountains to make it happen.

***

The whole house smells of Mom when I step inside. And not the warm-baked chocolate chip cookies, fresh apple crisps, honeysuckle shampoo in a wet head Mom, but the sweat-soaked, urine-drenched, drunker-than-a-skunk Mom. But the scent's stale, meaning she was in the living room and apparently has moved the party to the bedroom now. I'm too irritated to check on her right away, even though the music coming from upstairs is more annoying than the neighbor's dogs barking all hours of the night.

I can't believe she's this wasted, and it's not even three o'clock. After Robert and I left the pizza stand and he walked me back to my car, he invited me to his place that night. I was hoping Mom would still be sober when I got here, maybe agree to go out with a couple of her girlfriends from work so I could actually enjoy myself instead of the constant worrying I do when she's here alone. I guess I should call him and cancel. No way I'm leaving her alone in this condition.

I run a hand through my hair and drop the ponytail holder I just removed from it onto the kitchen table. I grab a can of soda from the fridge and turn on the television when I'm back in the living room. I wave a hand in front of my face, cursing the smell I know I'll be dealing with for the next forty-eight hours when I notice something else. It happens simultaneously: the smell of smoke hits my nose and the blast from the smoke detector rattles my ears.

"Mom!"

I take the steps two at a time, sprinting when I'm at the top of them. I bolt through her bedroom door. Everything's happening in a quickened frenzy and in slow motion all at once. I see her, seated cross-legged in the center of the bed, pictures of Dad and Paige scattered about her in their usual display. But this time there's a metal garbage can beside the bed, and she's dropping pictures into it one by one, flames and drunken screams of delight greeting them as they leave her fingers.

"Mom, what are you doing?" I yell over the blaring of the smoke detector.

"Burning the hurt away," she says. "Making it all go away."

I scramble to the hall closet to retrieve the broom. I have to kill the smoke detector so I can think straight. I glance in Mom's direction when I'm back in her room. She tosses a few more pictures into the burning trash can, but I simply let her. Part of me feels guilty because I know I should be trying to stop her. Why the hell am I letting her burn their pictures? But deep down, I know the answer. Maybe she's right. Maybe what she's doing will finally burn the hurt away. For years she's destroyed herself, destroyed me, and God knows that hasn't motivated her to get well. Maybe when she sobers up and realizes what she's done, she'll finally get the help she needs.

There's no time to climb on a chair and remove the battery from the smoke detector. I position the broom handle over it instead and whack it until the noise stops. I drop the broom and turn around, and that's when I see it. The edge of Mom's bedspread is on fire. I see her hands come down on the flames before I can stop her.

"Mom, no! Get away from it!"

Panic grips me, but I push forward. I smell her burned hands before I see them. She's screaming and I'm moving in auto-pilot, faster than her drunken state, quicker than the fire. I push her down off the bed and safely onto the floor on the opposite side of the flames. I race to her door and pull the fire extinguisher down from the wall it's hanging on. I've practiced this rescue a hundred times, always afraid she'd burn our house down from her drinking. I release the foam from the extinguisher onto the bed and then the garbage can. The fire's out in less than ten seconds, my dead father and sister's pictures now nestled in a sea of white foam and soot.

When the smoke reaches the hallway, the smoke detector hanging there bellows to life. I pull my mother into her bathroom and fill the sink with cold water.

"Put your hands in the water," I say.

She's mumbling something, so I do it for her. I shove her hands down in the sink and she cries out, but she leaves them there.

"That's right, Momma," I praise her. "Just leave your hands down in the cool water and I'll be right back."

I don't allow my own tears until I'm up on a chair in the hallway, yanking out the batteries in the smoke detector. I need to calm down, need to breathe. I take a few deep breaths and my lungs are ambushed with stale smoke air. My stomach retches.

"Anna, please help me!"

I'm back in her room in seconds.

"We're going to the emergency room," I yell. I grab her purse from the dresser. I know we'll need her insurance card and I.D. for the E.R. When I'm back in the bathroom, I wrap her hands in cold washcloths and we make our way out the door.

"I'm sorry, Anna," she keeps muttering between sobs. "I'm so sorry."

"Everything will be okay," I tell her, even though I feel like our whole world is falling apart.

***

The music's still screeching from Mom's room when I get back home. I never turned it off in our mad rush to the hospital. When I'm at her door, I divert my gaze from the bed and the disaster I know I'll have to face before the night is over. What if every picture is obliterated, destroyed beyond repair? What if the only one we have of— No, I can't think about it. I pull out my phone instead and scroll through my pictures. Fortunately, I have one of Dad that I copied from Mom's photographs. It's from a fishing trip he took when he was around twenty-five, and he just looks so happy and free. It's my favorite picture of him. But then the guilt hits me. I never bothered to take one of Paige.

It's hard for me to admit that at times I've been jealous of Paige. Well, not Paige exactly, but jealous of how much Mom loved her, how devoted she is to her memory, even to the degree that she's devastated our lives almost beyond repair. The thought of being jealous of a dead child makes me feel sick, especially now that I understand Mom's anguish better than I ever thought I could. Losing a child is unnatural, shouldn't happen...

My phone startles me. It's Robert.

"I got your message." He sounds panicked. "What happened?"

"Mom was drunk and had the bright idea to start a fire in a garbage can beside her bed."

"What the hell for?" His voice is strained and tight. "She could've killed you both!"

I hate the worry in his voice, knowing he can't bear the thought of losing me again. My own head was jumbled with similar thoughts while it was happening. But, honestly, I was more worried about losing my mom and having to bury her in the reserved patch of dirt beside Dad and Paige. It has always been my biggest fear, even as a little girl. What if I lost my mom? What would I do? Sometimes her drinking makes me feel orphaned and alone, but today I could've been orphaned for real, and it terrified me.

"Everything's all right now," I assure him. "Mom burned her hands, but she's going to be okay."

"What about you?"

"I didn't get hurt."

He doesn't sound convinced. "You sure you're okay?"

"I'm fine." *I'm lying.*

"So what did the doctors say about your mom's hands?" he asks. "Did they send her home?"

"No, she's still in the hospital."

"For how long?"

I put him on speaker and toss my phone on the bed when I'm back in my own room. "The burns weren't as deep as I thought. They're just keeping her overnight for observation. I was going to stay with her, but Mom insisted that I come home. I don't think she can look at me right now. She's too ashamed to even make eye contact with me."

"Well, maybe that's a good thing," he says. "Maybe this was the wake-up call she needed to finally get some real help."

"Yeah, I would say that burning the only photos we have of our dead family and nearly burning our house down in the process should be a pretty huge wake-up call.

If this doesn't motivate her to get help, I'm not sure what will."

"I would think that putting *you* in so much jeopardy would be the wake-up call she needs." Robert sighs, but then he's quiet. After a couple of seconds, he asks, "Did you lose all of them? The pictures, I mean."

I peek out of my bedroom door and across the hall into Mom's room again. I haven't been able to bring myself to really look at the chaos this afternoon brought with it. I'm too afraid to see if every original photograph we have of Dad and Paige are gone.

"I'm not sure," I say. "I hope I can salvage a few of them, at least."

"I can come over and help sort through things if you need me to," he offers.

"No, I'll be fine. And I'm really tired. I might wait and tackle it in the morning before I have to pick up Mom. I've already let the nursing home know I can't make my shift. I'll call you tomorrow though, okay?"

"Sure. Get some rest, my love. I'm so glad you're safe. Good night, Anna."

My heart's pounding so hard it hurts my chest, but I ignore it. I have to know if they're all gone, if the very items my mom treasured more than our lives are lost forever. I ease into her room like I'm walking on glass, wondering how I'll manage to even sleep here tonight with the God-awful smell that's still wafting through our house. I glance into the metal garbage can, but it's a total loss. Everything in it is long gone, so I don't bother to go through it. I pull it away from her bed and into the center of the room, a pitch black soot stain clinging to my fingers when I release my hold on it. It's obvious that getting this thing out of here will help rid the house of most of the smell, so I set to work. The sooner I get this over with, the better.

After a couple of minutes, I've scooped up every picture that's damaged beyond repair and tossed them into the burned garbage can. Thank God some of the pictures only had a few drops of the fire extinguisher foam on them, so I wiped the spots away and set them aside. I scour the remaining few, unable to control the tears now burning my cheeks when I realize a couple of her favorite shots are lost forever. How will she cope with the loss? What will she do? But when I'm at the bottom of the last small pile, I pick up the picture I was thinking of and fall to my knees. I can't stop the sobs that tear through me. It's unharmed, not even so much as a drop of foam or fire. And it's our absolute favorite photo of them.

And the only one of its kind.

The day before Mom was going to meet Dad and Paige at the restaurant to tell them she was pregnant with me, our next-door neighbor was playing around with his new camera and snapped a shot of Dad, Mom, and Paige in our back yard. Paige is hugging Mom's middle, her small hand on Mom's stomach like she knows her baby sister is nestled there, waiting to meet her. Mom determined that it is technically the only family photo we have, and she cherishes it more than anything.

I make my way back to my room with the photo and take a few pictures of it myself with my phone. I stand it up on my dresser and then busy myself with the clean-up once again. I managed to save sixteen pictures in all— sixteen sweet parts of the devastation we faced today that managed to survive, even though they should have been as lost as all the others. I renewed them, saved them...

And I'll save my mom, too, no matter what it takes.

LEE ANN WARD

CHAPTER 14

I concentrate on everything that Dr. Martine says, hang on her every word.

"You'll need wound care every afternoon for the next five days, then every other day until needed after that. You were very lucky, Ms. Berkeley. This could've been a whole lot worse."

"I know," Mom says. "Thank you, Doctor."

"You ready to go home?" Dr. Martine asks.

"Absolutely." Moms looks at her bandaged hands. The right one has a burn that covers half her palm, but the left one only has a spot about the size of a quarter. "Guess I'll be left-handed for a little while, huh?"

"Looks that way, but you should heal just fine." The doctor turns in my direction and smiles. "I trust you'll be a big help to your mom, right, young lady?"

The irony almost elicits a full-out belly laugh, but I refrain. "I will indeed," I say instead.

"Great." She turns to Mom again. "I'll get your discharge papers, Vikki."

Mom hasn't said one word to me since I walked in on her talking to the doctor about five minutes ago. Now that we're alone, that hasn't changed. I know she's embarrassed, completely humiliated for almost burning our house down yesterday. I don't pressure her to talk, so she simply mills around the room. First, she fumbles with the paperwork some other doctor left about caring for her burns, then she moves to the window and fiddles with the strings on the blinds. But when she opens the empty closet and simply stares at the coat hangers, I have pity on her and speak first.

"I can make us some brunch when we get home. I don't know about you, but I'm starving."

"I guess we have a lot of cleaning up to do when we get home, huh?"

There it is, finally—her attempt at damage assessment.

"I did that already. The mattress was only singed a little, thank goodness. I can't say the same for your comforter or mattress pad, though. I had to throw them out. I put on some new sheets and a blanket from the hall closet. They'll work fine until we can get you some new bedding."

"You're too good to me," Mom says. "You know that?"

The lines around her eyes are more prominent than usual, as if the fire aged her twenty years overnight. But I can tell by the anguish in her eyes when she looks at me that the fire isn't responsible for her appearance. Guilt is the thing that's consuming her. She's completely submerged.

Finally, she says it. "How could I bring myself to do such a thing? What was I thinking? How could I destroy all I have left of the two things I loved—" Her breath catches and her eyes dart in my direction again.

"Go on, say it." I hold her stare, refusing to allow her to look away. "How could you destroy all you have left of the two things you loved most in this world? That's what you were going to say, right?"

She lets out a breath like it's her last and crumples in a chair next to the window.

"My God," she says, "I *was* going to say that to you, wasn't I?"

She extends her least injured hand to me and I gently take it. She puts my hand against her cheek and holds it there for several seconds.

"How often do I say things like that to you?" she asks.

"Never when you're sober—"

"How about when I'm drunk?" Her voice is harsher, more desperate.

"A lot I guess, but it's—"

"What? Three or four times in a weekend?"

"Mom, it's fine, really."

"How many?"

"More times than I can count, okay! God, Mom. Why make me say it?"

I immediately regret yelling, and kneel on the floor in front of her chair. I lay my cheek on her knees like I did when I was little, and she scoops the sides of my hair into her bandaged hands, allowing the strands to fall softly, like she's handling spun gold.

"I'm sorry," she whispers. "So sorry, my sweet girl. I don't deserve for you to be my daughter."

"Please don't ever say that. Let's just focus on getting you well, okay?" My words feel squished because I don't dare move my head away from her knees. I'm enjoying her soft touch and the tenderness she's so freely giving me. God, I miss my mother. After a minute, she nudges me to stand.

"Could you bring me my shoes? I'm so ready to get out of here."

"Sure," I say. "I have something else for you, too."

I skip the shoes and go straight to my purse. Time to broker the deal I've been mentally preparing for all morning. I pull out the pictures I rescued and set them on her lap. All but one.

"Oh, Anna…" She turns the pictures around in her hands the best she can, surveying which ones I managed to save. I notice her face fall when our family shot isn't among them, then I pull it from behind my back and place it on top of the others.

"You need to get clean and sober, Mom. Yesterday could've killed us both. You need to get well and figure out a way to stay well."

"I know," she says.

I point to the photos. "Will you get clean and sober and stay that way? Will you do it for them?"

She covers the pictures with her burned hands. "No…no I won't." She locks eyes with me.

"But, Mom…why? I don't understand—"

"No, I won't do it for them…but I'll do it for you."

I wrap my arms around her middle, relief racing through my chest like wild horses. "Thank you, Mom. I love you so much."

"I love you too, baby girl, and it's about time I proved it."

***

We've been home for a couple of hours now. Exhaustion hasn't hit me until just this moment, but I push through the fog of sleepiness and meticulously scan every item Mom places in her suitcase. She's driving herself to rehab as soon as the packing's finished. This new facility is a couple of hours away, but the phone calls have been made and she's all set. They're admitting her this evening. I can honestly say that this is the proudest I've ever been of her. Although she's no stranger to rehab, this is the first time I've seen her approach it with nothing but gusto and absolute vigor. She wants sobriety this time. I can tell. I smile at the thought. Maybe this go-around, it'll actually stick.

"So I called my boss," Mom says. "I told her I was injured and released from the hospital this morning. She allowed me to take my three weeks' vacation I saved up starting tomorrow, so that all worked out well."

I nod. I know her. When she's nervous she prattles on and on, so I let her.

"I paid the bills that'll come due while I'm gone, so that's taken care of. That'll only leave around a hundred dollars in the account, but my paycheck will direct deposit on Wednesday. A hundred should be plenty for gas and food until my check deposits, huh?"

"More than enough," I assure her. "I'll be fine, Mom. I promise."

And I will be. This isn't the first time I've been left home alone for a few weeks because of rehab.

"Am I forgetting anything?" she says, eyeballing her suitcase before closing it.

"Just these." I place the remaining photos of Dad and Paige on top of her folded blouses.

Mom reaches around my shoulders and retrieves a framed photo of me from her nightstand. She sets it on top of the other pictures.

"Now I have everything." She winces when her burned hand brushes the top of the suitcase too hard.

"Oh," I say, "I almost forgot about your burns. You're supposed to have them cleaned and checked over the next several days. How will you do that now?"

"They have RNs onsite," she says. "They should be able to do my burn care, and if I get an infection or something, there's a hospital about a mile away from them. They said someone will drive me there if need be, so no worries." She glances around the room one last time. "I guess all that's left to do now is go."

My insides clench with nerves—happy nerves combined with good, old-fashioned nervous nerves. A lot's riding on this. I know it. She knows it. And I'm good with that.

"Come on," I say, glancing at her hands. "I'll carry your stuff to the car."

When we're outside, Mom lets out a long, slow breath.

I toss her bags in the back seat.

"Make sure someone helps you with those when you get there."

"I will," she says. She embraces me for several seconds before adding, "I can do this, you know."

"I know."

"I love you, Anna."

"I know that, too."

She nods and gets in the driver's seat, rolling down her window slightly. "Keep all the doors and windows locked," she calls as she pulls into the street.

I don't allow the tears to fall until she's driving away, and I watch her car 'til it's nothing but a speck of candy apple red against the gray-blue sky. Hope seeps into the void I've carried for so long now when it comes to her drinking. I sprint up the front steps, locking the door behind me. I fall on the couch and close my eyes, welcoming the first real sleep I've had in the last forty-eight hours.

***

A prickling awareness washes over my chilled skin when I wake up. I glance about the living room, dread filling me before I fully recollect yesterday's events. But the mini-panic subsides as I recall that Mom's at rehab. *Did I lock the door? What time is it? My God, how long did I sleep?* I glance at my phone. Five a.m. and at least ten texts from Robert. I know he's probably worried, so I send a quick reply letting him know I'm fine and simply fell asleep. I'll text him again when I know he's awake. Five a.m. leaves me plenty of time to get ready for school. I can't believe I slept for almost thirteen hours straight. But then again, I suppose it's the first real sleep I've truly had in months.

I eat cereal and finish the homework I thought I was going to have to turn in half-done. I throw on a skirt and top I'm not particularly fond of, but it's the only matching outfit I have clean at the moment. I'll have to do some laundry after school today, but no sweat. I spend a little more time on my makeup than usual, hoping maybe people will focus on my face rather than what I'm wearing. I grab my stuff, lock up the house, and climb into the Wombat. I put the key in the ignition and turn it, but nothing happens.

"Oh great. Come on, come on, baby. Not today. Just start."

I turn it repeatedly. Still nothing. *Super.* The Blue Wombat has officially bit the dust, and it couldn't have happened at a worse time. I sit for a moment, thoughts racing through my head that end up crashing and burning. How will I get to school? Or to the nursing home? I've heard Mom say a hundred times that my dad was great with cars—taught her how to change a tire on their third date. But she never bothered to show me how to do it, even when I asked her to. She always said, "I will one day, I promise."

But one day hasn't come so far. I feel like a little kid at an amusement park, standing in line for that one sweet ride I've been dying to get on for forever, only to make it to that stupid sign with the stupid lines saying "you have to be at least this tall to ride." I'm never tall enough, never allowed to ride. But I remind myself that Mom's finally in rehab—finally getting some help. And maybe this time when she finishes the program, she'll teach me how to change a tire.

I know Robert doesn't have his first class until ten, and I'm sure I'm waking him up, but I call anyway.

"Hey, Anna," he says in a croaking morning voice. "You okay? I was worried."

"My car won't start, and I'm pretty much stranded. Mom's in rehab a couple of hours from here and drove herself. I'm not sure what I'll do without my vehicle now that hers isn't here for back-up."

"Whoa, your mom went to rehab? That's awesome."

I love the true excitement I hear in his voice. "It really is," I say. "I think she's really determined to get well this time."

"That is so great, Anna." I hear him rustling around and feel guilty again that I've woke him. "Just give me a few minutes to get dressed and I'll come take a look at the car."

"You're a lifesaver," I say.

"Well, don't throw any praise my way just yet. I may not be able to do anything with it."

I doubt that. I'm pretty well convinced that Robert hangs the moon.

"See you in a bit," he adds.

"See ya."

***

I watch in fascination as Robert collects another wrench from his toolbox and goes back into the Wombat's hood for round two. No way I'll make it to school today, but it's okay. I can honestly say I've never played hooky in my life, and I guess this isn't technically playing hooky, either.

"Well, now I feel like an idiot," he says.

"Why?"

"The battery was the first thing I checked, but I forgot to check the terminals. One's bad, that's why your car won't start. It's an easy fix, though."

"Well, that's a relief," I say.

He sets to work again and I watch his every move, the way his muscles tighten beneath the white T-shirt I'm sure he'll have to throw away by the time he's finished with my car. A bead of sweat drops from one of his blond curls onto his neck, and my eyes follow it until it disappears against his shirt.

"There," he says. "All done. Let me just see if she'll crank."

"If *he'll* crank," I correct.

"Oh, begging your pardon, my lady." He winks. "I'll just see if *he'll* crank."

In seconds, the car starts and Robert smiles. "See, I'm good for something after all."

His phrase triggers another thought, and I can't hold back the laughter it provokes.

"What's so funny?" he asks.

"It's just that…in some of my dreams, I've watched you shoeing horses and repairing wagon wheels. And now you've fixed my car."

He laughs at the observation. "Yeah, we're something else, you and I. And I'll let you in on a little secret. When I was born into this time—a time with motorized vehicles— I have to admit, I wasn't hating it."

He busies himself with the car again, closing the hood and using the tail of his shirt to wipe an oil stain from the bumper. My head swirls with the dozens of questions I've considered since his arrival in this time. I know I should be thanking him for fixing the car, but I can't stop the words that come next. "What's it like? Waking up in a new life, but remembering all the other lives you've lived?"

He straightens and looks at me, his eyes so tender and full of love that I want to take him inside and kiss him until everything in the world goes away except for us.

"There's no warning," he says. "It's been that way each time. Death hobbles me in one life, and I awaken in another. Sure, I'm an infant, and I can't say that I recall being reborn or anything. But there is always an awareness, one that I can't explain. And then one day when I'm still quite young, the memories take over, possess my mind like a beautiful sickness…"

I hear him take in a breath, and chills tickle my arms when his lips part again. It's like he's on the edge of something so deep and haunting that even words can't accurately describe it. And so I wait for his prelude, his confession of a pain he's held inside for centuries.

"My memories simply rush in, Anna. They rush in like a flock of swallows, looping and twisting in a pitched sky that was once clear. Swallows make no announcement, give you no warning, whether there be fifty or a million overhead. They simply fill up the heavens with billows of black, and you stand there mesmerized, willingly captured in their majesty."

"Oh, Robert," I say, clasping his arm despite the oil and grime from working on the car. "I guess you do feel captured, don't you? It has to be beyond torturous, recalling everyone and everything you've lost in those lifetimes."

He takes my hands in his and I can feel his heartbeat in his fingers.

"Make no mistake," he says, "up until our wilderness days, the only person I grieved for from my previous lifetimes was you. That may sound cold, but it's true. But then we had the children, and I have suffered that loss from the moment I recalled them in this existence. And, Anna, a part of me is so glad that you are, for all intents and purposes, an only child."

I'm confused. "Why would you say that?"

"Because I was an only child too, until I was thirteen. That's when my parents had my baby brother, Matthew. When I saw him, he was the perfect reflection of Robert Jr., and I thought I was going to have a nervous breakdown, like the universe was punishing me for allowing our babies to—" He squeezes my hands tighter. "I was thirteen, Anna. Thirteen, but carrying all this inside me. There was no way I could tell my parents what I was going through, how I was feeling. My mom knew something was wrong. She wasn't sure what it could be, but she knew something wasn't right. She calls me an old soul. How's that for irony?"

I embrace the pain I see in his eyes as he speaks of our children. No way am I admitting to him that deep down, I'm still struggling with the fact that he drank himself to death when he lost me in the wilderness—that he wasn't strong enough to endure for the sake of our babies. As much as I love him, crave him like the air in my lungs, I wish he'd been stronger for them.

"But I guess I deserved for Matt to look like Robert Jr., to be a constant reminder. I mean, I'm the one who left them alone in that cabin. I'm the one who let them die."

My hands are on the sides of his face and my lips capture his harder than I anticipate. I want to extract the painful words, draw them out like venom until every drop of torture he's endured evaporates, melts away in the salvation of my touch. I need for his guilt and my own hidden blame to vanish. The real irony is this: sometimes love's a sickness, but only love can cure it.

In seconds, we're leaning against the car and Robert's breath is in my ear. "I need you, Anna, more than anything in this world."

"I know. And I'm here."

Suddenly he lifts me onto the hood of the car. He presses against me, my skirt pushed up farther than is decent and my legs dangling down on either side of him. I knit my fingers into his hair, his earthy scent of sweat and musk bringing me back to the wilderness, back to *my* Robert. He's more familiar to me now than in any moment in this lifetime, and if I don't know anything else, I know I want him—have always wanted him.

My lungs feel tight, like all the air around me is too thin to take in. But he's my air, my breath. I squeeze my legs against his hips, nudging him closer, even nearer to me. He responds, kissing me so deeply that I almost lose my balance. But his large hand finds the back of my head and entangles my hair, supporting my weight and his, but never breaking the kiss.

"I love you, Anna," he whispers against my lips. "I'll spend eternity loving you."

The sincerity of his words makes me shudder. "I love you, too," I say in a ragged breath. "Always and evermore."

He trails a finger along my cheek. "Do you know how much time I've spent missing this face, those eyes?"

I know how much time I've spent having visions of my past life and believing that Robert would forever be a memory, with no real possibility of being with me in the flesh. And I've watched my mom suffer for seventeen alcohol-soaked years without my dad. But I can't imagine what it's been like for Robert, loving me for spans of hundreds of years, only to lose me time and time again. And he did lose our babies too, has suffered as much as I have, and more. How could I know his true pain? How could anyone know? So I won't dare pretend to.

I say instead, "We're together now, and we're safe. That's all that really matters."

Robert's expression is solemn and serious, his eyes scanning the details of my face like he's committing it to memory.

"You know," he says, "there's always been one thing I can never make sense of, no matter how much I try rationalizing it."

"What's that?"

"I've never understood why every lifetime takes away the one thing that makes my life worth living."

His lips are soft and scorching, up my neck and against my shoulder before I can catch my breath. When his fingers find my thighs, he realizes just how far my skirt is pulled up, and just how public our display must be. His large hands tug my skirt down.

"Your virtues, my lady." Then he lifts me off the car to stand in front of him.

"And my virtues matter a lot to you, don't they?"

"Everything about you matters a lot to me. That's why I'm glad I was able to fix your car, and why I'm thrilled that your mom went to rehab. I want nothing but happiness for you, Anna. I want you to be so utterly, crazy happy."

When his lips find mine again, I explore the taste of him, trying to decide if his mouth tastes more like river water or raindrops. But it's neither. He tastes exactly like happiness…exactly like forever.

CHAPTER 15

"It's me," Robert says when he's at the door. I smile at his announcement. Who else would it be?

The last several evenings have been so blissful and perfect that sometimes I fear I'm merely dreaming of him again, so fearful of waking that I scarcely blink. Part of me feels guilty for being this happy, knowing that Mom has been detoxing hard over the past few days. But I was able to talk to her last night. The withdrawal has her miserable, but she's making it. Hopefully, the worst part of the physical pain will be over soon and she can focus solely on her sobriety.

"I'm sorry I'm late. I was working on something and got held up."

"It's fine," I assure him. "I was on the computer anyway."

"I know we wanted Mexican food tonight," he says, "but the line at Taco Bell was crazy long. I hope barbecue's okay. I got us a sampler platter from The Rib Shack."

"It's perfect. I love barbecue." God knows I couldn't care less what we eat.

We spread the food out on one end of the bar, and I

hop up and sit on the other side. Robert opts for a barstool and then grins so wide his face might break.

"What?"

"You," he says, "and how you still prefer to sit on every kind of furniture except a chair."

"What do you mean?"

"Well, in Canterbury, you always plopped your pretty little self on top of your dressing table to sit, and in London, it was the wooden fence rails enclosing the horse pasture. You were the only fine lady in petticoats who never minded getting your slips soiled or your hackles up when someone scolded you for it. Oh, but you loved your father's horses—always insisted on mending the lame ones yourself to spare them a sure death. And in the wilderness, you made a habit of sitting on top of your hope chest. But something told me you would." He winks. "That's why I made it so sturdy—"

"I had a hope chest?"

"Not just *a hope chest*," he says. "You had the finest hope chest in the territories. I mean, I built it, after all."

As much as I love his stories of our past lives, I wish I was like him and could remember more.

"I don't remember the hope chest. I want to so badly. I'm sorry."

He reaches up and lifts my chin. "Don't ever be sorry for not remembering something about our pasts, you hear me? I remember enough for the both of us, and I'll always tell you everything I remember. I promise. Now, let's eat. I'm starving."

After a few minutes, we're elbow deep in barbecue sauce. I flinch when I realize some sauce is on my cheek. I use a clean knuckle to swipe away the slight burn and tickle.

"Here," Robert says, tossing a napkin aside and standing. "Let me get that for you."

"I'm fine," I assure him. "It came off."

He retrieves a paper towel and wets it in the sink. He

dabs it on my cheek when he's in front of me again. "Your skin's always been so sensitive. I shouldn't have ordered the spicy sauce. My bad. There, it's all off now."

The sob his gesture triggers is stuck in my chest, but the tears fall just the same. When Robert notices, he freaks and I feel ridiculous.

"Oh, God, Anna! What's wrong?"

"Nothing, it's just…"

"Tell me."

"What you just did, knowing how sensitive my skin is, and wiping my cheek…my mom hasn't acknowledged my skin allergies in years, and she's never done anything as simple as wetting a napkin and wiping my face, not since I was a baby." I take a fortifying breath. "I'm always the one taking care of her…taking care of other people. No one's ever taken care of me. Well, in this life at least. Most of the time I feel like I'm the girl people pass along the way."

"Well, that's funny," he says, "because I've never been able to pass you by."

Within seconds, I'm in his arms. He swoops me from the bar and carries me to the couch, his mouth capturing mine as he lays me back onto a large couch pillow. He sighs against my mouth and I take in the soft heat of his breath.

His words are low and pressed against my lips. "If ever anyone has passed you by in this life, then I must believe that, somehow, they see your soul and know you belong with me. Most people are too afraid to touch a miracle. That's what we are, you and I. Miracles. But I promise you with all I have, you will never feel alone again."

The kisses he trails down my neck are dizzyingly warm. He traces my entire body from head to toe with the slightest graze of his finger and I arch my back in response. I've never wanted anyone or anything in my life except for Robert. That much I do know, even when I *didn't* know. He's right. For so long I was the girl who didn't believe in them or trust that they could ever be real.

But we are indeed miracles.

When his fingers come to rest on my chest, his hand just above my breasts, I tense a little and he notices. He kisses the end of my nose then offers a hand to raise me up from the pillow.

"Do you know what I want to do for the rest of the night?" he asks.

My heart's thrumming against my ribs, but I try to sound nonchalant. "What would that be?"

"Sit here on this couch with you, stuff our faces with popcorn, and watch movies."

I let out a breath I've been holding. "Seriously?"

His eyes soften. "Seriously."

I tangle my fingers in his and kiss his cheek. "Thank you."

As much as I want to be with Robert—to spend the rest of my life with him, however many that may be— we've still only been together briefly in this world, in this time. I want to take things slowly, enjoy getting to know the crazy-hot guy sitting next to me on the couch. I want to watch movies, go bowling, walk the mall and then talk all night until the sun comes up. I want him to take me to prom and on a road trip to the beach this summer. I want our modern-day fairy tale. God knows we deserve it.

I tuck myself under his arm and lay my face against his chest. He brushes a stray hair from my forehead, pressing a light kiss on it.

"You look tired," he says. "Are you comfortable enough?"

"Comfortable enough?" I repeat. "You know what? I'm perfect...this is perfect...we're perfect."

He grins and snuggles me closer. "Perfect, you say? I can agree with that assessment."

Everywhere I look there's a thin layer of frost. I can see it, feel it, touch it until the warmth of my fingers melts it away into oblivion. I'm in the cabin in the wilderness, but there's no fire in the fireplace, no wood on the stove. It's abandoned, empty. I've never seen it like this. I glance about, panic pricking my heart like the needling cold that's now working its way up my arms and the backs of my legs. I look down at my clothing, at the denim shorts and red cami that do nothing to protect me from the icy chill that's thickening the blood in my veins. I'm confused by my attire, but I focus very little on my physical discomfort. I continue moving forward. Where is he? What has he done?

"Robert!" I cry out, my breath as dense as fog when it meets the iced air. "Robert! Where are you?"

I'm met with dead silence, my words echoing back into my throat until it aches and throbs. The more I scream his name, the more my neck burns. I place a hand around my throat when I feel the trickle, the warm blood now dripping through my bare fingers and onto the floor. My neck is sliced from ear to ear. I recall Claude's face—my own kitchen knife pressed deeply into my throat. I let the recollection of my death seep through me, like the blood through my fingers and the chill now reaching my bones. I keep moving—keep calling out his name—keep searching for my husband.

I step into our bedroom, his name still falling from my lips. But he's not here. He's nowhere. I move on...

Dread fills me when I turn toward the doorway to my right. I will my eyes to scan the room, and they finally come to rest on Emily's cradle. My babies. Where are my babies? I move toward the cradle, and I see him. I'm paralyzed. Frozen.

It's Robert Jr.

I bolt toward the cradle, screams gurgling from my gashed throat in a fury of blood and panic. My son's blue face and frozen arms are clutched around his tiny sister. Realization tears my heart to shreds. My toddler son, cold and alone, must've climbed into the cradle to warm his baby sister, desperately attempting to shield her from the stinging cold. I touch their lifeless faces, still every bit as sweet as the day I gave birth to them. I'm not prepared for the pain that grips my core and ravages my dead soul like mangy vultures. I clutch my babies tightly, pull them to my chest, cry out with every scream and whimper my mangled throat has the power to release. And then, I let them go. I guide them back into the cradle, their icy frames now mingled with my blood and tears. I kiss their stone-hard cheeks then pull a small blanket up far enough to cover their breathless faces. And then it hits me. I dart out of the cabin without looking back. I remember where my husband is, what my husband did.

Robert is drunk.

Robert is in the barn.

Robert is dead.

I run far and fast—so fast that my breath stabs my chest like ice picks, but I ignore the pain. I'm focused only on Robert, on our dead babies, on the icy wilderness surrounding me, urging me to continue. I push the barn doors open when I reach them. My strength is waning, fleeting, seeping from my body like the blood from my neck. I spot him immediately, his lifeless form stretched across the dirt floor, his eyes gazing heavenward. An empty gin bottle is nestled against his side.

I lift the bottle and hurl it at an anvil, cursing as it shatters into thousands of splintered shards piercing the iced air. I fall on top of my husband's corpse, the familiar smell of urine and vomit assaulting my nostrils.

"Why?" I wail with a pain that cripples my senses. "Why, my love? Why would you do this? Our babies. Our beautiful babies, they need you."

My words echo off the walls. I am the only one who hears them, the only one who will ever hear them. I sob against his chest, holding him so tightly I can barely breathe. I grab a fistful of his blond curls, the hair so icy and brittle it feels like it's breaking in my hand.

"Come back to me," I plead. "This didn't happen...you

didn't let this happen. Please, Robert! I'm so sorry I died, but you have to come back. Please wake up and save our babies."

But he remains lifeless and still.

"Robert," I whisper into his cold ear, "please don't make me face this. Don't make me feel this. You have to wake up, do something."

But I *am* facing it, feeling it, hating it. I collapse across his body, totally spent, totally alone. I embrace the soulless shell of the only man I've ever loved, my tears meeting the blood that's still falling from my severed neck. I caress his frozen, handsome face and whisper against his cheek, "Our babies are dead, my love...and they're dead because of you."

I scream and awake with a start, still lying on the couch in the crook of Robert's arm. He startles, his eyes blinking to adjust to the lamplight, and then widening on me.

"Anna, what's wrong? Oh my God, are you all right? You look like you've seen a ghost."

"Not ghosts," I say. "I had a nightmare. I saw...I saw..." I push up from his chest, my hands clammy and shaky. I'm crying now, but I can't stop. I look at him, but all I see is the cabin, my babies, and him on the ground in the barn.

"What did you see?" he asks, rubbing my shoulders to calm me.

"I was in the wilderness again. My throat was slit, but I was walking around, dressed almost like I am right now. I found our babies, frozen and alone. They were dead. And then I found you, dead on the floor of the barn."

The horror I see in his eyes silences me.

"Oh, God. I'm so sorry, Anna. That had to be horrible."

"It was unbearable. I fell on top of your dead body, begging you to wake up and save our children. But the last moment of my dream was the worst."

His voice cracks. "What could be worse than that?"

I lower my head, not wanting to see his eyes when I say it. "I blamed you for all of it. I said over your lifeless body that our babies were dead because of you, and then I woke up."

"I'm so sorry," he says, his words just above a whisper. His face is a mixture of pain and humiliation. "Do you want me to go?"

"No," I say a little louder than I should. "Why would I want you to leave?"

"Because I've already told you how sorry I am, how ashamed I feel every day knowing that I abandoned them, that I died that night. I don't know what else to say, what else to do to show you how sorry I am. I would give my life to bring them back, Anna, to change what happened that night. You have to know that."

I lean in to him, wrapping my arms tightly around his middle. "I don't want you to go. It was a nightmare, that's all. None of us can control our dreams. We all wrestle a few ghosts every now and then. I'm fine, really."

We sit there in the silence for a few moments, then Robert looks at his phone.

"It's one in the morning, and you have to get up early. I need to go."

I don't argue with him, knowing that it wouldn't do me any good if I did. I walk him to the door and kiss him like I want the nightmare I shared with him to melt away into the moonlight.

"Sorry I ruined your perfect night," he says.

I bury my hands in his blond curls and tug his face toward mine. "You didn't ruin anything, you hear me? I'm fine. It was a nightmare. I'm good, really."

He nods and heads to his car, and I watch him drive away. I lied about one thing, though. I wasn't wrestling with ghosts tonight—I was battling demons. And demons are much harder to wrangle, a lot tougher to break free from. Demons aim to destroy, and they are masters at their craft.

CHAPTER 16

I have to be at the nursing home by seven. I opted to go in a little earlier because I promised Maggie I would go shopping with her today—a move I now strongly regret. I'm so tired I can hardly stand. Why is my subconscious torturing me, allowing me to have nightmares about my children's deaths? Why can't I have more past-life memories like before, happy recollections instead of the cruel images my mind's too vividly recreating? I retrieve the silver rattle and roll it in my hands, closing my eyes to the faint sound of clanking metal crying into my ears. I drag it harder across my palms, welcoming the haunting melody of a two-hundred-year-old toy, still weeping for my babies. I wipe my own tears and then put the rattle away, their tiny faces still consuming my thoughts.

I take a quick shower, get dressed, and pull my wet hair into a ponytail. Hopefully I can grab a decent breakfast before I leave. I startle when my phone rings. This is early, even for Mom, and I'm sure Robert's still snoozing away. My heart stalls when I see New York's name on the display.

"Is Rose okay?" I say instead of hello.

"Well, good morning, Anna. Calm down, child, I didn't

mean to scare you. Rose is fine, but she had a bad night. The overnight staff said she coughed a lot and didn't sleep much. Now she's just picking at her breakfast instead of eating it. I'm a little concerned, so I thought you should know."

"Thanks, New York. I'll see you soon. I was already coming in early today, anyway."

I send a quick text to Maggie and Robert, letting them know that Rose isn't feeling well, and to inform Maggie that shopping's out. I need to spend the day with Rose.

***

"Are you sure you can't eat just one more bite?"

Rose's cheeks are sunken in farther than usual, but she smiles at me with the alabaster teeth she's always been proud to say are her real choppers.

"Please stop fussing over me, Anna. I've had my fill."

I set the fork back on the tray in front of her and sit in the chair next to her bed. "Do you want to move to the window and people-watch?" I ask. "Lots of visitors today."

"That sounds nice." Rose nudges my hand away when I offer it. "I know I'm getting feebler by the day, but I can still get out of bed by myself."

That's the spunk I love seeing, so I allow her to stand without my assistance. I watch as she moves to the chairs in front of the windows, her frame noticeably more lanky and spindly. She's still in her nightgown, something Rose would never do if she felt better. She's way too proper not to have on a day dress by eight a.m. But at least she's wearing her jewelry, the chunky ring and long strand of pearls seeming monstrous on her tiny frame. The day I enter this room and Rose isn't wearing her jewelry will be the day I know she's truly ill.

"So," I say when I'm seated next to her, "I have some good news. My mom entered rehab last weekend."

168

"Oh, Anna, darling, that's wonderful. I'm so glad." She coughs then places a wrinkled hand on top of mine. "That makes me so happy. You deserve to have a healthy mother, especially after I'm gone."

"Don't say things like that. You're going to be around for a long time yet."

"I hope so," she replies, "but when it's my time, I'm not afraid to die." Rose looks me straight in the face, her eyes so full of shine they look like glass. "I've lived a good life, a happy life. And when I still had fire in my belly, I fueled that fire with the things I was passionate about—my music, my husband, my child. I've lived, Anna. Really lived, so I'm not afraid to die. Do you understand?"

I swallow the knot in my throat and cup another hand on top of hers. "I understand."

"Good," she says, "then you'll be really good at it, too." She notices my confusion and adds, "At living, my dear. You'll be really good at living."

When the serious moment passes, Rose dives headfirst into people-watching, first sympathizing with a man who's walking with a limp then pointing out a woman wearing a hat that's two sizes too big and *flat-out tacky* in her words. Then she directs my attention to something else.

"Do you see that flower? The one sprouting up between the cracks in the sidewalk?"

I follow Rose's bony finger in the direction she's pointing. "Yes, I see it."

"Well, I heard the janitor tell New York yesterday that he had to take care of that weed in the sidewalk. That weed just happens to be a Stargazer Lily that managed to push its way through a sliver of concrete just to make that beautiful flower for us. It's in the wrong place, but it's still a strong, majestic flower—not a weed. How could anyone mistake a lily for a weed?"

Her keen insight reminds me yet again why I love her so much. She coughs, and this time it sounds a little worse, a little deeper.

I kiss her forehead before standing. "Let me get you something to drink." I pour her some ice water from a pitcher beside the bed and hand it to her.

"Your beau is on his way in to see you," she says before taking a sip, nodding toward the parking lot.

"Well, just so you know, I texted him that you weren't feeling well. I'm certain he came to see you."

She smiles so wide her wrinkles seem to dance around her face. "He's a fine young man, and he loves you right and true, Anna. Right and true."

"I know," I say, leaning over her chair from behind and wrapping an arm across her shoulders and neck. I press my cheek to hers as we watch Robert walk toward the double doors leading into the building. I think about my nightmares from last night and admit, "But love's pretty scary, and at times it's downright awful. I mean, what if he completely shatters me, Rose, from the inside out?"

"Oh, but he will, my darling," she says. "And it wouldn't be love if he didn't."

"Knock knock," Robert says when he's in the doorway. "I heard this room was occupied by two beautiful ladies, and I couldn't resist checking it out for myself."

I meet him at the door and say into his ear, "I'm so glad you're here. She's feeling a little better, but I know you'll lift her spirits. It was so sweet of you to come."

"No way I wasn't coming after I got your message. I think Rose is awesome."

My stomach growls and Robert smiles. "Hungry much?"

"Starving. Would you mind sitting with Rose while I go to the cafeteria? I won't be long."

"Sure, but I can't stay long. I have a lab in about an hour and I can't miss it. I mainly just wanted to check in on her."

In two minutes I'm in the cafeteria, scarfing down a cheese sandwich and a banana. I grab some coffee to go and make my way toward Rose's room again. I stop dead in my tracks when I see someone else headed in that same direction.

"Well, hey, Anna."

"William? What…what are you doing here?"

"I saw Maggie at the gas station. I asked about you and she said you were at the nursing home this morning and that Rose is really sick. I was concerned. I hope you don't mind that I stopped by."

I let out a breath. "No, of course not. That was really sweet of you, actually."

"So, how have you been?" he asks.

"I'm fine." I scramble for anything to say, awkward nowhere near covering what I'm feeling at the moment. "Hey, I saw that you made the winning field goal against Brookwood last night. Congratulations. That's amazing."

"I appreciate that. You know, Anna," he says, "I really hate to lose."

We both turn when Rose's door opens.

"Hey, I better get going—"

But Robert's quiet when his eyes connect with William's.

William's face looks like a hand just slapped it. "Hey, uh, Robert, right?"

"That's right," Robert says. "What's up, man? Good game last night."

William cracks a half-smile. "Thanks."

In the next few seconds of uncomfortable silence I see realization pouring into William like water. There's no denying I'm Robert's girl, and he doesn't understand it.

"I really need to get to my lab now," Robert announces. He turns to me. "I'll see you this evening."

"Okay, sure." I widen my eyes to Robert and he catches on, opting not to give me a peck on the cheek for William's benefit. He makes his way to the double doors in front.

"So," I say to William, "would you like to go in and meet Rose?"

"Why?" he asks.

"What do you mean *why*? You came here to check in on her, right?"

"Not that." He pulls his fingers tightly through his scalp and shrugs. "No, I mean, why him? Why him and not me? Help me understand, Anna. Where did I go wrong with us?"

The thought of getting into the break-up with him again makes me queasy. I'm not going down that path with Will—not a second time. Not ever. So I tell him as much of the truth as I can.

"It's complicated, I guess, but we have a history. And being with Robert feels natural, feels right. I never meant to hurt you, but had we stayed together, I would've been stringing you along for nothing, and you would've ended up hating me. Robert was my first crush, my first real love…my only love. We both realized it when he came back and we met up. I'm not trying to be cruel, but you deserve to know the truth."

His eyes are cool and serious. "So tell me, what's the truth? Were you seeing him when we were dating?"

His words cut me to the bone. I never wanted to do wrong by him, not even with Robert, so I'm resolute. "I've only known you for a few months, William, but I've known Robert forever. Was I seeing him when I was dating you? No. But the truth is that I'm glad things didn't get more serious between you and me, because it never would've worked out for us."

He clears his throat and nods. "I hope he appreciates how lucky he is, then."

I spout the understatement of the century. "Oh, he does."

William nods and clears his throat. "Well, I'd still like to meet Rose, if that's okay?"

"Absolutely."

He follows me into Rose's room. After introductions and some small talk, Rose starts to nod off, so I help her back to bed.

"She didn't sleep much last night," I say to William. "She's just really frail now, it seems."

"Hey, not a problem. I've enjoyed talking to her. She's a nice lady." He glances at the clock on the wall. "You hungry? We could grab some lunch somewhere."

My face obviously lets him know where I stand on the suggestion, so he clarifies. "I mean as friends. Just food, nothing else. You have to eat, right? And if I remember correctly, you only volunteer 'til noon on Saturdays."

He's right, but I'm not leaving Rose today. "I think I'll pass this time. She had such a rough night, so I'd feel better staying here with her a little longer. But I appreciate the offer."

His eyes are steadfast on me, so much so that I feel the need to turn away, but I hold his stare instead.

"Promise me that we can still be friends." His eyes are soft, urging.

"I would like that, William, very much. But I still don't think having lunch together is something that's ever going to happen. If I run into you when I'm out with friends, then of course we'll socialize. But lunch one-on-one, it's just not going to happen. I'm sorry. I hope you understand."

But his eyes tell me that he's far from understanding, still trying to process why a girl like me—pretty in a classic way, but not particularly beautiful—broke up with the star athlete, the handsome hottie, the big man on campus. The guy like him. But that's just it. William was always way too intense, way too serious when we were dating. I'd never want to give him false hope, never want him to think that he has a chance with me. I wish with all that's in me that William would forget about me and move on. He can have any girl he wants. I just wish he'd stop wanting me.

He puts on his best fake smile. "All right, sure. I understand. I guess I better go now."

New York bolts through the door with her usual gusto.

"Anna, excuse me, sweetie. I know you're not on our time now, but would you mind serving dessert to the last five residents on this hall? We're really shorthanded today."

"Sure, I'll get right on it."

"You're a lifesaver. I'll just leave the cart here." She heads out the door again. "Thanks."

William notices when I glance in Rose's direction. "I'll sit with her 'til you get back. Go on. It's fine."

"Are you sure? It may take a little while—"

"Just go."

I head out of Rose's room, eyeing the food cart next to the wall. Dessert choices today: apple cobbler and peanut butter pie. I make the first three deliveries fairly quickly, trying to hurry because I know William is waiting for me to return before he leaves. All I have left is Ms. Beechum and Mr. Nathan. Ms. Beechum is particularly chatty today and keeps me at least fifteen minutes, so I'm thrilled when she becomes more interested in her pie than our conversation, and I excuse myself back into the hallway.

"Ugh, Mr. Nathan," I mutter when nature calls. "Lord, give me strength."

I decide to make a quick trip to the restroom before going into his room. I glance at the tray before parking it beside his door. There's two servings of apple cobbler left and one plate of peanut butter pie. I slide the pie over to the side and remind myself to wash my hands really well before giving him the apple cobbler.

When I'm done in the bathroom, I notice that the cart has been moved. I spy it at the end of the hall. One of the other Sunshine Warriors must've given Mr. Nathan his dessert. I scowl when I remember that the only other Warrior here today is Dustin. I don't blame the boy for wanting brownie points, but the least he could've done is take the cart back to the cafeteria.

I get behind the cart, then it happens simultaneously. I realize that the only dessert missing is the single slice of peanut butter pie, and I hear the horrible sound coming from Mr. Nathan's room. My heart stops for a millisecond. I rush to him as reality sets in. He's holding his throat and gasping, his lips and face so swollen he resembles a blowfish. The red signs in his room mock me. I know he's experiencing anaphylaxis.

I push the red button on the wall and grab the EpiPen from the drawer beside his bed. I throw back his covers and plant the injection against his thigh. After several seconds, some color seeps back into his still-swollen face and he's breathing a little better. Three resident attendants, including New York, rush into his room.

"My God, Anna!" New York says. "What happened?"

"The ambulance is on its way," another attendant named Sarah says. "They should be here soon." She turns to me. "I'm glad you used the Epi. You may have saved his life, by the looks of that swelling."

New York asks me again, "What happened, Anna? What did he come in contact with?" Then, she spots it. "Is that...?" She lifts the plate of pie from his nightstand. "It is. Anna, this is peanut butter pie. You gave him peanuts?" She points to the red signs around his room. "You know he's highly allergic, child. Oh my God—"

"But I didn't!" I say. "It wasn't me!"

New York's face falls. "But I asked you to finish up dessert on this hall—"

"And I did, but I had to use the restroom after I delivered to Ms. Beechum. Mr. Nathan was my last stop. When I left the bathroom, the first thing I noticed was that the peanut butter pie was missing. That's why I rushed in here and found him like this. I didn't give him the pie. Maybe it was Dustin—"

"No, Anna," Sarah interjects, "Dustin has been on my hall all day, playing checkers with Mr. Solomon. I know it wasn't him."

"Well, it wasn't me," I insist. "I would never give Mr. Nathan peanuts. I'm extremely careful with his allergies."

Just then the EMTs make their way into the room and

start loading Mr. Nathan up for his trip to the hospital. William steps into the room amid the chaos and questions that are still darting at me from every direction.

"What happened? Is there anything I can do?" William asks.

"Who are you?" Sarah says.

"I'm a friend of Anna's. I'm here visiting Rose. What's wrong?"

"You've been with Anna all day, then?" Sarah asks.

"Not all day," Will replies. "Actually, I was about to leave, but I offered to sit with Rose while Anna finished delivering desserts. Why?"

New York cups a hand over her mouth and Sarah scowls in my direction.

"But I told you already," I say, "I was in the restroom. I didn't give Mr. Nathan the pie."

"No one is saying you did it on purpose, dear," Sarah says. "People make mistakes—"

"It wasn't me," I say again. "I swear it! You know what, when he feels better, just ask him who gave him the pie."

In a couple of minutes, the EMTs are out the door and wheeling Mr. Nathan down the hall. They're taking him to the hospital for precautionary measures. He's breathing normally again because I was so quick with the EpiPen injection, but no one's acknowledging that now. New York and Sarah step into the hall, leaving William and me in Mr. Nathan's empty room for several seconds.

"What are they talking about?" William asks. "If you gave him the pie, it was an accident, and he's okay now. What can they really do?"

"Shh," I say close to his face. "I want to hear what they're saying."

New York steps back inside the room and Sarah proceeds to the office.

"Anna," she says, "please tell me the truth, child. No one will be angry with you. And I feel terrible that I didn't know peanut butter pie was on that cart. Did you give it to him by mistake?"

I clasp her hands and look her straight in the eyes. "I swear to you, New York. It wasn't me."

She pulls me into a deep hug. "Then I believe you, and I won't ask you again." She releases me and heads for the door. "And now I'm going to question everyone in this bloody building. And when Mr. Nathan feels stronger, we'll ask him who gave it to him, okay? We'll get to the bottom of it. We have to."

"What happens if we don't?" I say, New York reading my eyes like a book. "I told you to ask him, but we both know Mr. Nathan has dementia. What if he doesn't remember who gave him the pie? He can't remember his own peanut allergy, for God's sake. A year ago he would've never eaten that pie."

New York sighs. "If we don't find the person responsible, then the facility manager will have no choice but to place the blame on you. You'll be put on probation for two months, and get three demerits. But I'm going to try my best to see that it doesn't come to that, okay?"

I nod. "Okay."

New York leaves, hotfooting it down the hall, a woman on a mission.

"This can't be happening," I whisper. "This is not happening. On his bad days, Mr. Nathan barely remembers what he had for breakfast five minutes after I take his tray away. How's he ever going to remember who served him dessert after what he just went through?" Hot tears stream my cheeks, but I don't bother brushing them away. How can everything I've worked for be stripped away in a moment? I didn't give him the pie, and I did everything I was supposed to when I saw him in distress. The room is spinning. My world is spinning. Three demerits. I can't get three demerits.

"It'll be all right," William says when I sit on the bed. "You only volunteer here, anyway. So what if you're put on probation? It's not a real job. And, hell, you saved a man's life. That oughtta count for something."

"If I get three demerits, I'll lose my scholarship. The safety of our residents comes first, always. If any harm comes to them, then there are consequences, no matter who you are."

William gets a horrified look and then sits beside me. "Oh God, Anna. I forgot about the scholarship. I'm so sorry."

I lean into his chest, unable to control the sobs now shredding me. He wraps his arms around me, cradling me until I'm spent. How did this happen? How did my future get so bleak in one day?

CHAPTER 17

It's a weird kind of quiet, the quiet that envelops you when you're devastated. I'm sitting on a metal bench in front of the nursing home, waiting for Robert to meet me. More people hurry in and out, and I can hear every movement, even the ones that typically go unnoticed in our mad existence—the swish of their shoes, the small rocks crunching beneath the weight of their brisk steps. I hear the birds on the ledge above me, chirping soft, melodic notes to their mates in the nearby trees. I hear the leaves rustling in those trees as the wind whistles through their branches, limbs rocking and swaying. I hear it all, every tiny speck of sound, even though my own voice is screaming in my head. It's a haunting quiet, the quiet you hear when your whole world is falling apart.

Robert pulls into the parking lot of the nursing home, and I meet him at his car. I fall into his arms the moment he's standing in front of me.

"I got here as quickly as I could. What happened? Is it Rose?"

"No. Can we go to the pizza stand and talk? I need to get away from here for a few minutes."

"Sure."

His large hand finds the small of my back as he leads me across the street. He orders a pepperoni pizza and a couple of sodas and takes my hand when we sit down.

"Please tell me what happened, Anna. I'm worried about you."

I take a fortifying breath. "New York asked me to serve dessert to a few of the residents. I delivered to everyone but Mr. Nathan because I had to use the restroom first. When I got back, the cart wasn't where I left it, and the only piece of peanut butter pie on it was missing. Mr. Nathan is allergic to peanuts, so I rushed to his room. I still can't believe someone gave him peanut butter pie. I used his EpiPen on him, but they took him to the hospital. He's going to be okay, thank God, but when I told Sarah that I didn't serve him the pie, she didn't believe me. New York believes me now, but she said if no one comes forward, I'll lose my scholarship."

"Can't you all just ask him who gave it to him?"

"Of course they'll ask him, but it's not that simple. He has dementia, and the early signs of Alzheimer's. It's very likely that he won't be able to tell us who did it. That's why he ate the pie in the first place. He can't remember what he's not supposed to have."

"But they can't do that," he says. "You've worked so hard for that scholarship. How can they just accuse you of something you didn't do?"

"I'm not saying that they won't ultimately take my word for it, but I'm scared. My stomach's been in knots all afternoon. I mean, if they can't get to the bottom of it, if no one else owns up to it and Mr. Nathan can't remember, then what can I do? I was the one New York asked to make the deliveries, and we were shorthanded today. My first thought was Dustin. He's the only one close to competing with me for the scholarship, and we were the only two working today. But Sarah says he never left her floor, that Dustin was playing checkers with one of the residents when it happened. There are witnesses to prove it." I rub my forehead to relieve the throbbing pain. "I can't lose my scholarship, Robert. I just can't."

He grazes a thumb over the top of my hand. "I know, but it hasn't come to that yet. They'll find out who did it. I can't imagine anyone there wanting to pin something on you that you didn't do. And since you and Dustin were the only volunteers, that means it had to be one of the paid employees. I'm sure they'll own up to it. Everything will be all right, you'll see."

I want with everything I have to believe him, but I saw Sarah's and New York's eyes today when Sarah was questioning me. Even though New York is standing by me now, deep down I'm sure she's debating my innocence. She knows how desperately I need that scholarship. And when I think about it being a paid employee, I feel sicker.

"But why would a paid employee jeopardize their job to get me off the hook?" I take a sip of my soda. "I'm so scared no one will ever set things straight."

Robert gets a determined look, like he's trying to fill in the blanks. "Okay, so you and Dustin were the only two volunteers there today. Who else besides New York works that floor?"

"There are several other nurses, but it's hard for me to imagine any of them giving peanut butter pie to Mr. Nathan. You have no idea how paranoid they make all of us when it comes to his allergies, and now I know why, firsthand. When I saw him like that today, turning blue and struggling to breathe, I was so scared. If he hadn't responded to the injection so quickly, I'm not sure what I would've done."

He rubs my arm. "I know. You did great with him." He clears his throat and gets back to business. "Listen, have they hired anyone new?"

"Not that I know of."

"Were there any other people on the floor, like family members visiting the residents?"

"A few. William said the same thing, that maybe

someone's relative took it upon themselves to bring him dessert. I don't know about that, though. Seems crazy to me."

"William?" Robert says. "William was still there when it happened?"

"Well, yeah. I mean, he was about to leave when New York asked me to make the deliveries, but he offered to sit with Rose until I finished. Why?"

"No reason, just curious is all."

We eat our pizza in silence for the next few minutes, Robert's brow denting the whole time like he's in deep thought.

"What is it?" I ask when he starts to look as far away as the moon. "What're you thinking about?"

"I have a theory about the pie situation, but I'm trying to be as tactful as possible."

"I'm listening."

"I think it was William."

So much for tact. "Robert, you can't be serious."

"Oh, I'm very serious," he says. "Look, we both know the guy still has the hots for you. His showing up today probably had more to do with seeing you than checking in on Rose. And when he saw me there, that had to sting. What if it's as simple as William trying to impress you by making your last delivery for you really fast when he saw you go into the restroom? He wouldn't know about that man's allergies—"

"There are red warning signs posted everywhere in his room. No peanuts. You'd have to be blind not to see them."

Robert sighs. "Even so, if William was trying to surprise you, he'd be as quick as possible and probably never notice the signs. And even if he did, he wouldn't know to check the flavor of the pie. That's why it would make more sense to be someone like William, someone who doesn't work there. I'm not saying he caused the man harm on purpose, I'm just saying that I think it's a big possibility that he did it unknowingly and then chickened out on telling anyone when he saw the trouble it caused."

"But William came into the room when the EMTs were working on Mr. Nathan, and when Sarah was questioning me. He knows what I have to lose if the responsible party isn't found. Had he done it, he would've spoken up right then. I know it. It wasn't William. He'd never hurt me like that."

"But it hurt him when you broke up with him, right? So, how do you know he wouldn't—?"

"Robert, what we've been talking about up until this point is someone accidentally giving Mr. Nathan peanuts, but what you're suggesting now is that William is being deceitful *on purpose*. Pretty harsh, don't you think? And you don't even know him."

"And you do? You've only known him a few months, right?"

"And I've only known you for a few weeks."

I regret the words the moment they fall from my lips. Robert looks like I just hit him in the jaw with a crowbar. Hot tears sting my cheeks as I try to backpedal.

"I'm sorry. I didn't mean it."

He half-smiles and swipes my tears away with his thumb. "Don't cry. It's all right. I know you didn't mean it. You've always been plucky, and so incredibly strong. Your strength is one of the things I love most about you. I'm not trying to be harsh concerning William, just weighing all the options. I know it's hard for you to imagine, especially since your heart is made of solid gold, but people do deceitful things every day. Even people you trust."

I can't believe Robert thinks William would do something like that, but I'm not getting into it with him now. I've let my mouth run away from me, and this day has been too insane already for me to squabble with him over something so ridiculous. I wish I could just blink and wish this whole rotten day away.

"I'm sorry I said that. You know how I feel about you.

I love you, Robert, and of course I've known you for more than a few weeks. You're all I've ever known."

"Don't apologize." His eyes are as warm as his kisses. "It's okay, really."

"If you don't mind, I'm going back across the street to check on Rose, and then I'm going home. I need to be alone right now. I hope you understand."

"I do." He lifts my hand to his lips and places a soft, gentle kiss on top, then he brushes the stray hairs away from my face. "You've been alone for a long time now, haven't you? Taking care of your mom, not letting anyone on the outside know just how rough you've had it. Today was soul-crushing. I get it, and I wish I could do something to fix it, but I promise everything will work out. I know it, can feel it. Call me if you need anything, okay? You never have to be alone again unless you choose it. I love you, Anna."

"I love you too, Robert, so much. Thanks for understanding."

When I stand to go, he pulls me tightly against his chest. When my gaze meets his, for a moment I forget that I'm falling apart, forget that my dream for college may remain just that, a dream. I forget that Rose is getting sicker by the day, and that my mom is miles away. All I see in this moment are his eyes, his face, his promises that everything will be okay. When he nuzzles his mouth against my own, my breaths slow and my stomach tingles. But his very public kiss is short.

"Be safe," he says against my lips, and releases me again.

I head for the nursing home without looking back, my rambling mind once again on Rose, my mom, and my broken dreams.

***

I wake up in the gray hour just before dawn. At least

184

that's how I recall Robert describing it in one of my flashbacks of our wilderness life. And the description has never been more appropriate. Everything about my restless night has been gray, dark, depressing. I've tried thinking of any possible way to determine who really gave Mr. Nathan the pie, in case he can't remember. I have a sick feeling that New York didn't get anywhere when she questioned the staff, because she never called me. I pull the covers tighter against my chin and let the realization sink farther in. No one's going to admit it. I'm not getting the scholarship.

When the first bit of sunlight creeps into my window, my feet hit the floor. I'm sick of lying in bed, thinking. I wish I could turn my brain off, stop the spinning images from swirling in my head. How do I tell my mom that I lost my scholarship? Should I wait until she's out of rehab, or tell her now? Is it too late to apply for other scholarships? Maybe I could look into grant programs...

No, I'm not doing this now. I have to stop obsessing over yesterday and get a grip, which is really hard to do when I know I'm losing control. That's what the Sunshine Warriors program has always been for me—control in a life where I've had none. I couldn't control coming in to this world with a dead father and sister, or the fact that my mom tried for years to drink her pain away, heaping it on me in the process. That was the one thing my wilderness dreams gave me—escape from reality when reality became too much to handle. But the flashbacks of my former life appeared when *they* chose to and have never given me any true sense of control. But the Warriors were different. Being a Sunshine Warrior was *my* decision, *my* choice. And working toward that scholarship has always made me feel like I could control my destiny, no matter if everything around me was falling apart.

I focus on my phone when it rings, thrilled to see New York's name on the screen. "Hey! So, do you know who gave Mr. Nathan the pie yet?"

"Anna," she says, her voice soft but strained, "I got a call about five minutes ago. The paramedics just left with Rose. You need to get to the hospital as soon as possible. She's not doing well."

I'm not breathing, not moving.

"Do you need me to come drive you, child?"

"No," I say. "I can drive myself. Thanks for letting me know."

"I'm so sorry, Anna," she says. "I know how much you love Rose. She loves you too, and she's strong. She may pull through this bad patch." She's quiet for a few seconds, then adds, "I'll see you later today, okay?"

"Okay."

My throat's so tight I can barely breathe, and my eyes are blurry with tears. I fumble around the nightstand for my keys but don't find them right away. I take a few deep breaths to calm the sick feeling when it hits me, then I grab my stomach and sink to the floor. I want to scream, need to vomit, try desperately to force myself awake so this isn't real, isn't happening. It's me and Rose against the world. I tell her everything, even the stuff I don't share with Mom or Robert. And more importantly, she shares her soul with me, a soul that feels so similar to my own that we've finished each other's sentences more than once. Sometimes I feel like Rose has been my only saving grace.

And I need her grace.

I need her smile.

I can't lose Rose.

***

Rose is in the ICU, but I'm allowed to see her, even though it's not officially visiting hours. They say she's been asking for me, but I know what's really going on before the doctor says a word. Rose is dying, and I'm here to make sure she doesn't do it alone. So I'm standing outside her door, too afraid to go inside, too terrified to move. But when she starts coughing, I go to her like I have a hundred times before. I've shared Rose's life since the day we met. I've applied her knowledge in several situations and listened to her stories about her family, her passions, her life. I've watched her live, marveling at her wisdom and strength. And now that she's coming to the end of her legacy, I realize that I love her enough to watch her die, too.

"I'm here, Rose. Let me get you some water."

"Anna," she says, her voice hoarse and weaker than usual. "I'm fine, really. Just sit with me. I need to tell you some things, and you have to promise to listen—to let me finish—no matter how hard it is to hear."

"I promise," I say, unable to keep my voice from cracking.

She coughs again but accepts the water this time when I offer it. She takes my hand and I have to fight back tears. She's not wearing her signature chunky ring, and I rub the spot on her finger where it has left its mark. Just like she's left a mark on my heart.

"They made me take off my jewelry," she says. It's in a plastic bag in the closet. I want you to take it with you when you leave."

"But you can put it back on when you get better—"

"Anna, I want you to take it with you when you leave. Promise me."

Somehow I manage, "I promise," from a throat that's swallowed a stone.

"Now listen, there is a beige lace dress hanging in my closet back at the home, and the jewelry that complements it is hanging with it on the same hanger in a pink pouch. Send that to the funeral home with me—"

I can't control the sobs and don't try to. She's shredding my heart. "Rose, please, I can't do this—"

"Oh, my sweet child, you're the only one who can do this for me. My dear, precious Anna. You're my family. You're strong." She squeezes my hand. "We can do this together."

I put on the bravest face I can muster, her confidence in me fueling my courage. "Okay. Beige lace dress. Got it. What else?"

"My funeral has been arranged for quite some time, so there's nothing for you to do. Just send the dress. And I know the home will expect my room to be cleaned out promptly after I'm gone. Promise me you won't forget the box in the bottom of my closet. It has my sentimental items in it, and now they're yours."

I nod, unable to respond with words. Rose coughs again, and her eyes glass more than usual.

"All right, enough with the business. Come closer, let me look at you."

I lean as close to her face as I can manage, and she touches my cheek. Her eyes are scouring my features, as though she's committing them to memory for a long journey—a journey from which there is no return.

"I'll miss your face," she says. "That's what I hate the most about this, how much I'll miss you, Anna."

"I don't want you to go, Rose." I know I sound like a child, but I don't care. "Please get well. Please don't die."

"My body's tired, spent. I'm not getting well, Anna. The sooner you accept it, the better. I've accepted it, and I'm ready to be with Ted and my precious Teddy again. I need to be home…need to be with them. You can understand that, right?"

I swallow back tears. "I do."

Rose's breathing slows and a machine starts beeping. A nurse comes in and checks it, and then secures the oxygen tube in Rose's nose.

"I'll get the doctor," the nurse says and then wriggles a finger in my direction. She leans close to my ear. "If there's more family that needs to see her, you need to call them now."

"I'm all she has, her only family."

The nurse squeezes my arm and nods. "I'm so sorry.

I'll be right outside the door if you need me."

"Anna, come here," Rose says, her voice weak and trailing.

I take her hand again. "I'm here. I love you, Rose."

"I know, child. And if I get to live another life, I hope you're there. I love you, Anna."

She never says another word. It took twenty-eight minutes and eighteen seconds for Rose to die after saying my name. I know because I counted.

CHAPTER 18

"You hungry?" Robert asks. "Sarah just dropped off another casserole. We'll never eat all this, but it was nice of the ladies you work with to bring so much food over."

"It really was," I say. "I'll stick most of it in the freezer, though, so it won't go bad. Rose's funeral was nice, don't you think?"

He kisses my forehead. "It really was, and very befitting a woman like Rose." He touches my neck. "I think she would like it that you wore her pearls."

"Me too," I say. "You know, it's funny, but I started volunteering at the nursing home to earn my scholarship, and now that it's gone, I have no regrets. I'll never begrudge a single hour I've spent there. I'll leave that place with so much more than I ever imagined. I met Rose, and she was worth it all."

He tugs me into his arms. "Just when I think I couldn't possibly love you one drop more, you say something like that and I fall hopelessly in love with you all over again."

I press my head into his tight chest and gaze up into his face—the only face that's ever made me feel dizzy, causing the entire planet to sway like he's the only real thing that exists in it. The kiss that follows is just as dizzying, just as intense. When our lips part, I try to breathe normally, a shaky glimpse of his mouth welcoming me to kiss him again, so I don't protest.

He whispers against my cheek, "You will never know how much I love you."

Robert lifts me into his arms and carries me to the couch. He lays me back on the cushions, both of his hands on either side of my face as he hovers just above me, his lips so near mine I can feel his breath. I close my eyes and allow my body to rule my mind. I'm tired of thinking, tired of waiting. When his lips graze my ear and cheek, I focus on nothing but my Robert from the wilderness, and then on my Robert that is here with me now. And I need him with me, need his closeness, need to be loved by the only man I've ever known.

I tug at his shirt and start unbuttoning it. He clasps my hands and stops me.

"Anna, are you sure? We don't have to do this now. I know how upset you are about Rose. We can wait until you're ready, until you're sure this is what you want and how you want it to happen."

"You're what I want, the only thing I've ever wanted, even before I knew you were real and seeking me out. I've been waiting for you my whole life, Robert Grafton. You're all I am, all I know. The whole world is right when I'm with you."

He allows me to unbutton his shirt this time, and I slide it from his shoulders. As I do, something falls from his pocket and lands in my lap. I pick it up and roll it around in my fingers.

"What is it?" he says, his breaths heavy and urgent as his kisses find my neck again.

"It's an acorn," I say. "I noticed a few falling from the oaks in the cemetery. This one must've found your pocket."

He pulls his attention from me to the acorn, a look of concern lining his face. He searches my eyes, and I know why. The memory he's recalling is one I've seen in my flashbacks as well.

"Acorn buttons," I say.

"Acorn buttons," he repeats.

I was stitching a new coat for Robert Jr., and the buttons I was using strongly resembled the caps on the tops of acorns. One day when I was less attentive to my sewing, Robert Jr. found the last two loose buttons I needed to sew on his coat, and he started playing with them. He lost them outside, so I attached a couple of buttons that didn't match the others. A few days later when he was playing outside again, he found some acorns and was certain that the caps matched the buttons on his coat. He was so disappointed when I explained that I couldn't sew with acorns that Robert made him a wooden dog, and I stitched it a tiny coat with Robert Jr.'s acorn caps for buttons. He loved that wooden dog with the acorn buttons, so much. Our sweet little boy...

Robert stands and slides his arms back inside his shirt. I know the moment's over, know that our shared memory is more than painful for him—for both of us. And as much as I want to tell him to come back to the couch with me, a part of me knows that I still hold him responsible for the deaths of our children, even if he never intended for it to happen.

"I'm sorry for bringing that up," I say, standing to meet him in the middle of the room. "You know, I am a little hungry. Maybe we should eat something—"

"Never apologize for loving our children, for remembering things about their lives. I'm the one who should be apologizing to you. Don't you think I know that? I should be apologizing every day for allowing them to—" But he doesn't finish the sentence. "I'm so sorry, Anna. I don't know why I drank so much that night. It's just that, after you died, every time I looked in their tiny faces, you'll never know the guilt I felt. At times I could almost hear them thinking that it was my fault you were gone. My fault that they didn't have their mother. I should've forced Claude to kill me instead. I never should've let him get close enough to harm you. It was all my fault."

I touch his shoulder and make him look at me. "Nothing Claude did that day was your fault. You have to know that."

He rubs his thumb over my cheek and touches my neck. When I wince, he grimaces.

"You're the sweetest thing that's ever happened to me, Anna, and it kills me knowing that your neck still feels the sting of his knife. I swear to you with all that I have, I'll make everything right somehow. I want to be a better man. I'm trying so hard, so very hard. You believe that, don't you?"

"I do," I say. "With all my heart."

He kisses my nose and buttons his shirt. "It's been a hard day. How about I let you have some privacy? You need to get some rest."

"Robert, please don't go."

A smile lights his eyes. "I'll be back tomorrow afternoon when you get out of school. I have something I need to take care of, anyway. Don't tell me you don't need sleep."

I *do* need sleep, but I hate this—hate making him feel so guilty.

"Good night, Anna," he says and heads for the door.

"You know I love you," I say before he's outside. "To the moon and back."

"And I love you through space and time, my sweet Anna. Forever and always."

When he's gone, I put all the food away and change into my sleep pants and a T-shirt. I climb into bed with my laptop and go to his Facebook page. I scroll through his drawings of me until I'm looking at the one from the wilderness. I stare at that Anna until my eyes burn, begging sleep to find me.

***

I hug New York when I see her.

"Hey, Anna. How was school?"

"Fine. How's everyone here today?"

"Oh, the usual. They've really missed you, though."

I'm not sure if she's saying it to be nice, but it still makes me smile. "Well, I'll be here bright and early Saturday morning. I guess I need to go finish up with Rose's room now, though."

She takes my hand. "I figured that's why you were here. You already have most of it, sweetie. There's just two small boxes on the bed and a box in the closet. Need some help?"

"No, it's fine. I've got it. Thanks, New York."

She winks, and I head down the hall toward Rose's room. It's still weird when I step inside and there's only blank walls staring back at me. Rose loved brightly colored artwork and photographs, and they had filled her walls like grand awards, treasured reminders of a life well-lived. But now the things that surrounded her daily are all packed up in boxes—boxes I'll carry to my car and put away in the attic. They're pieces of her that I'll never let go, even though Rose told me that most of her things were only fit for Goodwill or a garage sale. Well, I'm not parting with a single speck of her. I carry the boxes from her bed one by one and put them in my car.

I make my way to her room one last time. I still have to get the box from her closet, the one she said holds her sentimental items. I've had to muster the courage to look inside it. Losing Rose still hurts so much, but I need to know what's in that box before I store it, so I open the closet and set the box on the bed. I take a couple of deeps breaths and yank on the tape that's obviously kept it sealed for years now.

I'm met with piano books when the box is finally open.

One's so old that I'm almost afraid to touch it. The pages are yellowed and brittle, and a corner breaks off in my hands. I gently lift the four books and set them on the bed. I gasp when I see what appears to be her son's baby book, then I notice her and Ted's wedding album. There's a copy of *Little Women* that appears to be old as well, so I eagerly flip to the copyright page. It was printed in 1941. I imagine her as a young woman herself, reading it for the first time. The thought is so poetic that a shiver races up my arm. I pull more items from the box.

When I'm near the bottom, my hand brushes the top of something hard. I push aside a scarf and lose my breath. A hand flies to my mouth and I back away. For a moment I'm paralyzed, can't speak, can't move. My thoughts scatter in every direction. I inch my way to the box again and lift my own music box from it. My shaky fingers trail across the etching on top, carved delicately into the wood by Robert's strong hands. I open the lid and sob when the music-maker plays two short notes. But there is something different about the box. It is lined with red velvet that is visibly old and wearing. I examine the velvet's flimsy texture, then rip at it feverishly. Then I see it, the engraving Robert told me about. I mutter the words, *"This box belonged to Anna Grafton. Pass it to her only daughter, Emily, and all who follow in her line."* Is it possible? Could Rose be my descendent? She would've never realized it without knowing what was under that velvet lining.

And if Rose is my descendant, that means my babies didn't die in that cabin! Somehow, some way, they were rescued. Emily's box, my music box, was indeed passed down her line from generation to generation. No wonder I had such a strong bond with Rose. If the box was indeed passed to her, then she's my great- great- great- however many greats granddaughter. It just has to be so. We didn't die out in that frozen wilderness. Against all odds, our babies survived.

"Thank you, Rose," I say, clutching my music box so

tightly my knuckles are white. I pack everything away again, and set my music box on top of the pile. I make my way down the hall and to my car without anyone noticing my tears. I start the car and take my first real breath in days. I have to get home. I have to show Robert.

***

Robert's standing on my porch when I pull into the driveway, but I don't see his car. He's holding some papers, a smile stretched from ear to ear. I leave everything in the car and meet him.

"Where's your car?" I ask when he's within earshot.

"At my apartment. I walked to the campus library, but when I found what I was looking for, I just took the bus here. Anna, you're not going to believe it." He hugs me so tightly I can barely move. "I have something incredible to show you."

"You know, I was about to say the same exact thing to you."

"Me first," he insists. He leads me to the porch swing and we sit. He places the papers on my lap and points to them.

"What am I looking at?" I ask.

"A genealogy study. I didn't want to tell you I'd been doing some digging, just in case I didn't find anything. But I did find something. Anna, I found our children."

"What?" I say, my smile now matching his.

"Well, I know how crushed you've been, how hard it was for you to accept what we thought happened to our babies. I wanted so badly to show you how much I love you, how much I loved them. I started thinking about everything surrounding your death, and something occurred to me. There was a neighbor who showed up at the cabin a few days after you'd passed. She had a newborn son of her own, and she offered to take Emily home with her...to be our daughter's wet nurse. I refused to let her do it. You see, I knew that this woman and her husband had four sons already, and she desperately wanted a daughter. A man I was making a cabinet for had pointed this woman out to me in the general store. So, naturally, I was too afraid that if I allowed Emily to go, I would never get her back.

"This woman was very persistent, though. She came calling several more times, insisting that the goat's milk I was feeding Emily wasn't enough nourishment for her, that I wasn't tending our daughter properly. Her accusations angered me, but I remained the gentleman. I kindly thanked her for her offer but escorted her to the door, each and every time. I remembered her name— Claire Garvey. And I remembered her saying to me, 'Albert doesn't mind a smidge if I tend your wee one for you.' So, I started an ancestry search on Albert and Claire Garvey, and look what I found."

I read the names branching out from Albert and Claire. It lists their sons, Albert Jr., David, Johnathan, and Fredrick, and then I see it. It lists their adopted children, Robert Thomas Grafton, Jr. and Emily Lucia Grafton.

"Oh my God," I say, clutching the paper like it's a life ring and I'm drowning. "She saved our babies."

"That she did," Robert says, his eyes brighter than I've ever seen them. "God love that nosy, pesky, bothersome woman. She saved our children. And look at this…"

Robert lays a printout of an old photograph on my lap and I gasp, tears streaking my cheeks. It's a photo of the Garvey children…and Robert Jr. and Emily are in it.

"My babies!" I cry out, relief washing my soul like holy water. "Look at my precious babies." I've never beheld anything as sweet and beautiful in this life. "Oh, look at them."

"They're every bit as gorgeous as their mother," Robert says.

"I beg to differ," I say. "Our son just so happens to be the spitting image of his father."

"How old do you think they are there?" Robert asks.

"I'm guessing around nine and six." My eyes never leave the image now cradled in my hands. I mutter to myself, "Nine and six."

"And there's more." Robert places another paper on my lap. "I followed our children's histories as far as I could, and they both married and had children of their own. Our children lived, Anna. Meaningful, fulfilling lives. They lived."

"Well, I suspected so, my love." I smile and hand the papers back to him.

Robert looks confused when I stand up.

"Wait here," I say.

"Anna, where are you going?"

"You'll see."

I retrieve the music box from my car, but cover it with one of Rose's scarves before walking back to the porch.

"What do you have there?" Robert says.

"Another reason for us to thank that pesky woman for being so nosy. Apparently she cleaned out our cabin as well." I set the music box in Robert's lap. "Have a look."

He lifts the scarf, his brown eyes widening and glassy with tears. "Oh my God, Anna!" His voice cracks, but he makes no attempt to hide his emotions. "Where did you get this?"

I say four simple words. "It belonged to Rose."

I watch his expression as he works it out, loving the way his tears shine and the corners of his mouth turn up.

"She was ours?" he says, opening the box and running his fingers over the words he'd etched so very long ago. "The music box was passed to Rose because she was of our line?"

"I believe so," I say. "Someone had lined the box with velvet, so Rose never saw the etching. But I believe in my heart it was given to her on purpose. But following our children's genealogy a tad more would help us know for certain."

Robert's eyes connect with mine. "I don't need to follow it. I know in my heart she's ours."

I smile. "Me too, and maybe deep down, I always knew."

"Oh, Anna...thank God."

After a few minutes, we're in my bedroom with my music box softly playing on the dresser and the photo of our children propped against it. The genealogy materials are spread across my desk.

"It's like a dream," I say. "A wonderful, fantastic dream." I take Robert's hands in mine. "I still can't believe you did all this...found an actual photo of our children."

"My only regret is that I didn't find it sooner. It kills me to think about all the pain you've endured, thinking them frozen or starved—"

"Shh," I say. "Let's never speak of it again. Just hold me."

I step back so I can see his face—his beautiful, ever-familiar face. I run a finger along his jawline, the light dusting of beard tickling my hand. His jaw clenches at my touch, but I don't stop. I'm never stopping again.

"I want you, Anna. I need to love you, need you to love me."

"No words, then," I say against his ear. "Love me, Robert."

He lifts me and wraps my legs around his waist. He carries me to the bed and lays me back. He's over me, supporting his weight with one hand and tugging his shirt off with the other. I run a hand along his chest and stomach, his skin tightening beneath my touch. His lips feather mine, his kisses soft but full of heat. His kisses trail from my cheeks, down my neck and to my chest, and in one swift motion, he lifts me to a seated position. I watch him shrug off his jeans and boxers, and I'm mesmerized by the fact that everything about him is exactly the same, right down to the lone freckle gracing his right hip.

"Hold your arms up," he says.

I do, and he pulls my shirt off and tosses it to the floor. He rubs his hands over the straps of my bra and then the tops of my breasts. I draw in a breath when his fingers slip underneath the fabric. I lie back again, his lips now running from my breasts to my stomach, then my thighs and my legs. It's like he's thirsty and my skin is his only source of water. He tugs off my skirt and panties in one motion, and I'm dizzy. Every sensation in my body heightens when his hand spreads across my hipbone and the tops of my thighs.

And even though I'm still a virgin in this life, I remember every detail—the way Robert has always made me ache and burn, his narrow man-hips centered squarely over my middle, his gentle coaxing and soft caresses. I know this man, and I've dearly missed him.

"Slow at first, my love," he coos into my ear when I feel his manhood against my softness. "I'll never hurt you. I love you beyond measure."

I trust him, love him, want him more than I've ever wanted anything in my life. A moan escapes my lips when I'm finally one with him, my body melting into his, the motions slow and controlled. But when his need becomes too great, I wrap my arms around his shoulders, my fingers sinking into his back. I close my eyes to fireworks and lightning bolts, the sun and the stars, and every source of light that has ever been or ever will be.

I love this man beyond all reason. He feels like the end of a long journey home, like waiting your whole life for something that you've always known could be, and then finding out that he has always been. He is living and dying, being reborn and repeating. He is everything and sweet nothing. He is all of that and more.

***

I dangle the orange slice over Robert's mouth, moving it just out of reach when he lunges for it. He tickles my stomach and I squeal.

"Okay, okay, you can have it!"

"You shouldn't tease me with food," he says. "After all, it's your fault I'm so hungry."

"That was amazing," I say. "Is it always that amazing?"

"The first time? Absolutely. And I should know. We've had lots of firsts."

"Yeah, but you're the only one who can remember them all. How unfair is that?"

"Oh, unfair now, is it? I'll give you unfair," he says, tickling me again.

Robert glances at his phone when the playful torture ends. "Oh, it's seven already. I guess you need to take me back to my apartment. I have a paper to write for English."

"Oh, I forgot. You don't have your car. When's your paper due?"

"Tomorrow."

I shake my head. "Boys…"

"We can grab a bite to eat first, though. That orange didn't do it for me."

"All right," I say, "just let me change my clothes."

I stand to go change, but Robert catches me by the hand. "Wait, I want to give you something."

I can't imagine what it could be. He reaches into his jeans pocket and pulls out a gold ring.

"Here, this is for you. Read the inscription."

Etched on the outside of the band are two hearts intertwined. Engraved on the inside are the words *Love is Always Enough*.

"Oh, Robert. It's beautiful."

"It's a promise," he says, "a promise that I'll always love you. Anna Lucia Berkeley, I've asked you to marry me in every lifetime, and I'll ask you in this one, too, when the time is right. What's so grand is knowing that we have all the time in the world." He touches my face. "We'll actually get to grow old together now, and I'll see wrinkles on this beautiful face some day. We'll live, and live, and live. I love you, my Anna."

"I love you too, Robert. So much."

He slides the ring on my finger and I slide my arms around his neck. But before our lips touch, we're both startled by a knock at the door.

"Who could that be?" he asks.

"I don't know."

He looks down at his bare chest. "I'll go to your room and grab my shirt."

I notice William's car out front and answer the door.

"Hey, Anna." He looks me over and adds, "You weren't asleep, were you?"

"What are you doing here, Will?"

He's fumbling for words, so I wait a few seconds. He takes a deep breath and blurts, "Okay, listen. I don't know how to say this exactly, so here it is. I'm the one who gave the pie to Mr. Nathan."

"What?"

"Well, Rose was asleep and I was bored, so I watched you going from room to room. When you missed his room, I thought it would be okay if I gave him dessert. I was trying to help you out. But then you came back, and you rushed into his room so panicked. I freaked out when I realized the mistake I'd made, what was happening to that old man. I felt so bad, and I was scared I'd get arrested or something for giving him his food since I didn't work there. Hell, I'd never even been there before until that day. I hated them accusing you, but I was too afraid to speak up. And then when you reminded me about your scholarship, I felt so guilty…

"Anyway, I went to the nursing home today and spoke to the lady in charge of the Sunshine Warriors. I told her it was me, explained everything. So, she removed your demerits. You're still the frontrunner for the scholarship. I'm so sorry, Anna. Please forgive me for not admitting it sooner."

As much as I want to be mad at William, I'm so relieved to have my scholarship back that I throw my arms around him instead. "Thank you so much, William! I thought we'd never get to the bottom of it. I can't believe I have my scholarship back. Thank you."

"You're welcome," he says, his arms tightening around me.

"Well, hey," Robert says, walking up behind me. "How goes it, William?"

William's so surprised that he releases me and steps back. "Oh, I didn't realize you weren't alone, Anna. I'm sorry." All at once he seems to notice the ring on my finger and take in the reason I looked so sleepy when he arrived. "I didn't mean to interrupt," he says, "I just wanted to let you know about the scholarship and tell you I'm sorry."

I turn to Robert. "William accidentally gave Mr. Nathan the wrong pie. He told the coordinator, and I'm getting my scholarship back. Isn't that great?"

"That's fantastic," Robert says. He extends a hand to William.

William takes Robert's hand to shake it, but he holds the handshake a little longer than normal, his eyes widening as he looks in Robert's face. Robert breaks the hold.

"We'll see you around, okay, buddy?"

"Yeah, sure," William says, staggering back a little and then heading toward his car.

"Wow, he sure was surprised you shook his hand," I say to Robert when William pulls out of the driveway. "I think he thought you'd punch him instead."

"Well, I'd look that way too if I ever lost you," he replies. "That's worse than any old punch to the face."

I wrap my arms around his middle. "You were right about William all along. I can't believe he was the one who gave Mr. Nathan that pie. Your theory was wise—like, King Solomon wise. How did you do that?"

"I've lived a very long time, Anna. You pick up a few things."

I smile when I think about the scholarship again. Then I think about Mom getting clean and Robert here with me. My future's bright, and I'm happy. So incredibly happy.

CHAPTER 19

It feels like it's been forever since I've seen Mom. Robert, in his infinite sweetness, offered to drive me to the rehab facility for a visit. I called Mom about Rose, but I still haven't told her about the Mr. Nathan situation or about Robert. No time like the present, though. I want my mom well, want both of us to be whole. So, no more secrets.

"You nervous?" Robert says.

"A little. Why do you ask?"

"Because you're pacing."

He takes my hand and guides me to the bench beside him. "It'll be all right. You'll see."

We're seated in the gazebo area on the grounds of the facility, and I'm watching the double doors to the building like a hawk. And when Mom steps through them, I let out a breath. She looks healthy, younger, her cheeks a natural pink that I haven't seen in months. I can feel the tears, but I don't care. I know immediately that she's clean.

I run to meet her. "Mom! You look fantastic! I've missed you."

"I've missed you too, sweet girl." She backs me away so she can look at me then pulls me into a hug again. "I'm so glad you're here."

We join Robert on the gazebo and Mom extends a hand in his direction. "Hello, I'm Vikki."

"Robert," he replies, his weight making the wood floor of the gazebo creak when he stands. "It's so very nice to meet you."

She has a bit of a weird look at first, then sits and turns her attention fully on me. "So, how are things at home?"

I tell her all about the Mr. Nathan incident, how William finally confessed and now I'm on track to receive the scholarship again. She's totally rapt, hanging on my every word.

"I'm sorry I wasn't there when all of that was going on," she says. "I'm so sorry, baby."

"Well, everything worked out in the end, and I'm so glad you came here. You look incredible, Mom. Tell me about this place. Do you like it?"

"Actually, I do. I hated it at first when I was detoxing, but now it's so much better. The counselors here are brutally honest, and they challenge me in ways no others have. They've allowed me to open up—to really look at what my drinking has done to me, to us. And I don't want to be that person anymore. I want to stay clean and be the mother you deserve. I know it won't be easy, that I'll have to work on it for the rest of my life, but I know now that I can do it. I love you, Anna."

"I love you too, Mom."

"And, you know," she says, "I was going to wait until graduation to tell you, but I think now would be a good time."

"What?" I can't imagine what it could be.

"Well, your father and I set up a savings account for Paige when she was five. We wanted it to be used for her education. After she…well, I never could add as much as your father and I did when he was here, but I've added a little to it every year since you were born. It's not a ton of money, but the account does have almost eight thousand dollars in it, and it's yours for school when you need it." She smiles and takes my hand. "Surprise."

"Are you kidding me?" I'm so shocked I'm nearly speechless.

"Nope, I'm not kidding. I'm so proud of you, Anna."

I just can't believe it. "Thank you, Mom, so much."

We chat some more about the college money, then I take a deep breath and let the words I've been dreading all morning come out. "Mom, I need to tell you something else, and I want you to promise to be open-minded about it, okay?"

Mom gets that weird *my-child's-about-to-lay-down-the-hammer-on-me* look, but I keep talking.

"There's something I need to tell you about Robert, and I know it's going to be almost too unbelievable for you to accept, but—"

Mom looks at Robert. "What's your last name?"

He's surprised for a moment then says, "Grafton."

Her eyes widen, but she simply shakes her head. "You're the young man from Anna's dreams, aren't you?" She's visibly shaking. "How can that be?"

Robert stops me when I start to answer for him. "I honestly can't tell you why or how, Ms. Berkeley, but I can tell you that Anna and I have lived every lifetime together. She only recalls our life in the Michigan Territory in the 1800s, but I remember all of them. And I love her fiercely."

"Every lifetime," Mom mutters, trying to absorb his words. She's quiet for a moment, simply nodding like she's accepting something she always knew could be.

"Mom, I know this is a lot to take in. I was honestly surprised when you asked Robert his last name. I didn't think you'd remember it."

She looks hurt and I immediately feel guilty.

"Anna, do you really think I never listened to you when you told me about your dreams? I can assure you I heard every word. They consumed you so much that I was afraid somehow they'd suck you in and I'd lose you, too. I can even recall the time I realized you'd stopped sharing them with me. I know you did that out of love for me, but you know what? You never have to cut any part of your life out for me ever again. I'm here for you totally from this moment on." She looks at Robert again. "I'm not going to lie and say I understand any of this, but I'll try to. I promise."

I smile and choke back tears. My God. I have my mother back.

"I have another confession to make, too," she says. "Even before you had your first dream, you had some indication of a past life, and you were only three or four years old."

"What do you mean?" I ask.

"When you were very young, you used to always say, 'Mommy, I washed the dishes when I was big,' or 'I swam in the river when I was big.' And once, you even told me that you had a different mother when you were big, and that you had a father. That's when I lost it. I discouraged you from saying such things, and that was a mistake. I guess eventually you forgot those past-life memories after I no longer allowed you to speak of them. But the universe found a way to bring them back, and in a huge way. I'm just sorry I was so sick, wasn't nearly as supportive as I should have been. I'm so sorry, Anna."

"That was the past," I say. "Let's just focus on the future."

She smiles and looks at Robert. "Promise me one thing, young man."

"Anything."

"Since we've worked so hard on college for Anna, don't go running off and discouraging her from attending, okay? Both of you have your whole lives ahead of you."

Her mention of the future turns up the corners of Robert's mouth. "I promise. And will you promise me something, Ms. Berkeley? Will you promise to crack the whip on Anna when it comes to her grades and never allow her to slack up one bit in school? She gets lazy with math sometimes."

Mom laughs. "Don't I know it?"

I lightly punch Robert's arm. "Hey, I'm sitting right here. Rudeness."

We spend the rest of the morning catching up, the two people I love most in the world getting to know each other. *Perfection.*

CHAPTER 20

I head for the school parking lot as soon as fifth block's over. I need to pick up some groceries before heading home. I'm making dinner for Robert tonight, and I still haven't decided on what I want to cook. When I reach the Wombat, I notice a piece of paper stuck under one of my windshield wipers.

Meet me at the Spot at 3:00 ~Robert

A handwritten sticky note. Old school. I like it. I shove the note in my pocket. I start the Blue Wombat. "The Spot it is, then."

Within minutes, I'm pulling onto my street. Robert's car is already in my driveway, so I park behind it. I put my phone and keys in my jeans pocket and head to The Spot.

Robert's standing along the tree line when I reach the clearing. He's holding a piece of notebook paper. He smiles but looks like he's wound as tight as a spring.

"Hey. Sorry I'm a little late," I say. "Are you okay?"

"I'm great." He touches the wisps of curls around my face and the small braid that's trailing down one side of my hair. "I like it," he says. "It suits you."

"What do you have there?" I point to the paper.

He takes a deep breath. "I have something to tell you, something I've needed to tell you for a long time now, but I can't say it." His dark eyes are fixed on mine. "Here, take it." He hands me the notebook paper.

I laugh at the immaturity, not a feature I've ever seen in Robert. "You need to tell me something, so you wrote it down instead. And you want me to read it, in front of you? Awkward, no? Why don't you just tell me?" I clasp his hand, threading my fingers through his. "You should know by now that you can tell me anything. It'll be fine. I promise."

"You don't understand," he says. "I wrote it down because I'm too afraid of what might happen if the words are actually spoken out loud. But I promised to tell you everything, and that's exactly what I'm doing. After you read it, we should never speak of it again—not ever. I just need you to know it for yourself so there's never any secrets between us. I love you, Anna, and I'm trying to save us all."

"All?"

He folds his arms in front of his middle like he's bracing himself. "Please, just read it."

My eyes scan the paper furiously, his written words assaulting me like fists to the face. I gasp, a hand covering my mouth and tears moistening the paper.

"This can't be," I say. "It's not true."

His jaw clenches. "It is true. Every word. I'm so sorry, Anna."

"But, how can—?"

"Shh," he cautions. "Don't say it."

I'm angry, sick. Why is he telling me not to talk, not to say out loud what he's just confessed? Is it because he thinks the confession can be acknowledged, absorbed, and then simply crumpled up and tossed away? No, we have to discuss this. I need answers.

"Robert, how can you expect me not to have

questions? We have to talk about this!"

"No, we don't. Anna, please. You don't understand."

"Then make me understand!"

He reaches for my elbow, but I yank it away. Tears flood my face as I read the letter again, trying to piece it together, trying to make sense of it all.

"Why can't we talk about it?" I ask again.

"Because the dynamics are different this time. Please, Anna, try to understand."

My voice is raw and tight. "How are they different?"

"They just are."

"How?"

"Because you know me! You remember the wilderness and he doesn't! He's never remembered any of it, not in any lifetime. If we talk about it now, how do you know it won't spark some kind of recognition for him as well? I know it sounds ridiculous, but I'm not taking any chances, Anna. I won't."

The guilt hits me the moment the explanation leaves his lips. He has to think of every scenario when it comes to us, our safety, our future. So I nod, my eyes falling on the paper again, trying to soak in each word letter by letter. My head's spinning, the realization of the horror he's endured, that we've both endured in every lifetime, causing my stomach to churn. When I've read all I can fathom, I take his hand.

"Let's go back to the house," I say. "I'm thirsty."

"Okay. I'm glad you wanted to meet here, though. This place made it easier to bolster my courage, somehow."

I look him dead in the face. "It was your idea to come here, Robert." I pull the sticky note from my pocket. "You left this on my car."

He reaches into his shirt pocket and pulls out a similar note. "No, Anna. You left this on mine." He grabs my hand, terror lining his face. "We have to hurry! Run!"

We dart for the trail, but we see him at the same time. Robert pulls me to a dead stop. Someone's standing at the mouth of the trail, holding a gun.

And that someone is William.

"I have one question," Will says, aiming the gun squarely at Robert's chest. "How did you pretend not to know me, Robert? Was it just a game for you?" Then he looks at me. "And you, were you just planning to settle for good ol' William in case lover-boy here didn't show up in this lifetime?"

"I didn't know about you, William. You have to believe me. The only people I remembered from my past life were Robert and our children. I swear it!"

"The letter you were reading, read it aloud, Anna."

I glance at Robert.

"Read it!" William demands.

"Go ahead," Robert says, "It's all right."

I pull the letter from my pocket and toss it on the ground. "Read it yourself."

William chuckles, his eyes never leaving Robert's face and the gun never budging from its mark. "You see, Anna, I'm kinda busy here. Pick up the damn letter and read it, or I'll start blowing off parts of your boyfriend, bit by bit."

"Why are you doing this, Will? It doesn't have to be this way."

He aims the gun at Robert's knee. "One…two…"

"Okay, I'll read it! Please stop!" I bite back tears as I pick up the letter and clear my throat.

My dearest Anna,

I need you to read this to yourself, never uttering a word of this letter aloud. I am only revealing this truth to you because I cannot carry a lie throughout this lifetime. I was telling you the truth about your deaths in all our lifetimes, but what I haven't told you is that there is another person repeating. I'm sorry I haven't told you until now, but like yourself in every other lifetime, he has never remembered our past lives. In every one of our lifetimes, I swear I've tried to be a better man. I've tried to save us all from the tragedy that finds us, but I have to tell you now that the other person repeating with us is

William.

In Canterbury, William was the young man you were dating before we met, and it was William you were trying to save when he fell from that hayloft. In London, you were betrothed to William.

It was his blade you were defending me from when he ran you through, killing you and our unborn child. And William was the second horseman you saw riding away after he led Claude to our cabin in the wilderness.

William has been your jilted lover in every lifetime, and even though you only dated him briefly in this one, I want you to be cautious around him. I feel in my heart that the world we live in now has evolved enough for us to be safe, but it will never evolve enough for me not to be honest with you. I promise to be the man you can trust with your life, and I will give you all that I have, including the truth. And now you have it.

I love you for eternity and beyond ~ Robert

Now it's William who's fighting tears, a thundering yell pouring from his chest when I finish the letter. "All I saw was the wilderness," he says. "But there were others?" He aims the gun at Robert's head. "You've stolen her away from me in every lifetime, you selfish son-of-a-bitch!"

"No!" I scream, jumping in front of Robert when I fear he'll be shot. "And you weren't in every lifetime, William. Robert once said that one of the guys was named Adam—"

"That was still—"

"Shut up!" William screams at Robert. "Don't tell her. Let's see if she figures it out."

I search Robert's face and William finally blurts out, "Wow, did you care anything about me at all when we were dating?"

I'm confused. "Will, my God, what are you talking about?"

"My middle name is Adam." He aims the gun at Robert's head again.

A large hand grasps my arm when I step in front of

Robert for a second time. "Anna, move!" He pulls me behind him and William laughs.

"Still willing to die for him, I see. Why, Anna? What makes him so much better than me? Why don't you tell me? What!"

"How did you know about the wilderness?" Robert asks William, obviously trying to discern his intentions.

William's face twists into something resembling a smile. "You think you're so smart, not talking about our past lives with Anna. But you're not as smart as you think you are."

"How so?" Robert replies. "What did I forget?"

"You shook my hand the other day. When our hands touched, glimpses of wilderness flashed in my mind. I didn't understand it at first, but over the next few days, memories returned. I saw myself with Anna. I saw myself happy, happier than I had ever been. And then I saw you. You stole her away from me, just like you're trying to now. Well, not this time. I'm never allowing you to take her away from me again."

"It was never like that!" Robert says. "I never stole her from you. Had Anna ever once loved you, I would have stayed away. You never claimed her heart, William. Don't you see that? And this wheel of life that spins us back to this exact moment in every lifetime can end right here, right now. But not this way! That's why I wrote the letter. I'm not trying to hurt you, William. I'm trying to save you...save us all! If you put the gun down now, you can simply walk away and we'll pretend this never happened. I'm begging you, William. *Please*."

William laughs. "You're begging me? Perfect. Do it again."

"Please, William," Robert says, the desperation in his voice audible. "Please put the gun down and walk away."

William's laughter morphs into anger. "Walk away? Why? So you can ride off into the sunset with Anna yet again? No, not this time. I will not be the loser in every lifetime. Besides, I hate losing. I'll never allow you to have your happily ever after again."

My voice is soft at first. "Oh, but you're mistaken. We've never had the happily ever after, and it's all your fault." I'm not sure where I find the courage, but I push myself in front of Robert again, staring into William's gun like it's a toy. "And for your information, I was never yours to take. Not then and not now. I've seen the wilderness, too. It's the only lifetime I remember living besides the one we're standing in now, and I never recall seeing you in it. Well, except for that one time…"

"What time was that?" William says, searching my eyes like he's about to leap inside them.

"The one time I saw you riding away after you'd pointed out our cabin to Claude. Oh, and I do remember Claude. He put a knife to my throat and then slit it clean through. And I died, right then, all the while staring into my little boy's angelic face. Did you know Claude would kill me? Did you ask him to do it?"

"No, no, it wasn't like that!" William's eyes are wild, like a madman's. "Robert's polluted your mind, seduced you, and stolen your love away from me! I asked Claude to kill *him*, not you. And I helped string the bastard up for doing it."

"You're sick," I say, barely able to stomach the insanity he's spewing. "And Robert has never stolen me away from you. I'm with him because I love him more than you will ever comprehend. I love Robert, and only Robert—in this life and the next. The sooner you accept it, the sooner we can move on. Or do you plan to simply kill me again in this life? You have to know deep down that sooner or later, this has to end."

William's brow is soaked in sweat. "Well, how about sooner, then?"

He aims the gun at Robert.

"No!" I scream, throwing myself in front of him again.

"Anna," Robert says, his voice like velvet and fire.

"You've given your life for me twice already. I'll not allow you to do it a third time. I couldn't bear it. I love you with all my heart, my sweet Anna. Now move out of the way."

In one swift motion, he shoves me to the ground and lunges at William. They struggle for control of the gun, William's height giving him a slight advantage, but Robert's love for me keeps the gun in check. I fumble in my pocket for my phone and manage to dial 911.

"Please hurry! You have to help us! A guy attacked me and my boyfriend with a gun and he's trying to kill us. He's fighting with my boyfriend now. Please hurry!" I give the dispatcher the address and tell them how to find us down the trail, then I set the phone down without turning it off.

William frees the gun and I panic. Robert lunges for him again and I hear the explosion in my ears. I can't feel my hands, my legs. Everything's turning in slow motion. Robert staggers but grabs for the gun, with such force this time that he gains control of William's hands. He turns the gun on William and fires. William takes a bullet to the throat and I know he's dead before he hits the ground.

"It's over," I say, walking toward Robert. "It's over."

He drops the gun and then falls to his knees. That's when I notice the blood that's pouring from a hole in his chest. Robert's body hits the ground and I throw myself on top of him.

"Anna," he says, his voice making a gurgling sound. "I'm sorry. I tried to save William. I never…wanted this."

"Shh," I say. "Stop talking. You need to save your strength."

I tear open his shirt and scream when I see where the bullet has pierced him. I shove his shirt and my hands in the hole, trying desperately to stop the bleeding. I yell so the 911 operator will hear me. "My boyfriend's been shot in the chest! He's losing a lot of blood." And then my voice breaks. "Please hurry!"

Robert looks in my eyes, his now faraway. "I'm glad it's me this time. I can't live another lifetime without you." He uses what little strength he has left to touch my face. "You'll have wrinkles in this lifetime, my love. And when I awaken in a new life, you'll be there." He coughs and I scream.

"Please, Robert! Hang on! Someone's coming to help us!"

"You have to let me go now. I love you now and forever…my Anna."

His hand drops from my face, and I fall into his chest. I can't feel his heart, only warmth and a poisoned sea of red. I cry out his name until I'm spent. I try to breathe into his mouth, but there's nothing. He's gone and I'm screaming, his name still on my lips when I see the cops coming down the trail.

CHAPTER 21

I can't feel anything, not the breath in my lungs or my heart in my chest. I'm hollow, empty, nothing. I close my eyes and see his face, but I can't touch him. He has melted away into dust, and I want to die with him. The world around me continues to turn, people moving back and forth. They talk to me, try to comfort me, but I can't hear their words, can't feel their warmth. I have nothing left for them. I shouldn't be here.

I should be with him.

"Get up, Anna," Mom says, pulling back the curtains and bathing the room in sunlight. "Get up, now. You have to eat something."

"I'm not hungry," I say. "Go away and leave me alone."

She yanks the covers back. "I said get up. You haven't left this room in three days. You can't miss school Monday, Anna. Another absence and you won't pass this semester. Look, everyone has been so gracious about Robert, but your principal can't allow you to miss another day. Do you think that's what Robert would want? You throwing away everything you've worked so hard for? I think you need to go to the nursing home this morning.

It'll do you good to get back into your old routine. And it's a gorgeous Saturday. Maybe we could have a picnic in the park later…"

She's talking, but her words hit the walls, the floor, the brick-solid air that doesn't fit in my lungs anymore. I don't know what she's saying, can't focus on her sounds.

"Anna," she says, taking my shoulders and forcing me to look at her. "Did you hear me?"

I say just above a whisper, "I can't breathe." Then I find my voice, my pain, my anger. "I can't breathe! I can't breathe! Don't you get it? He's not here, and I don't know how to breathe anymore! Momma, he's dead. My Robert is dead."

Sobs tear through me, every drop of the pain I've been bottling up for the last couple of weeks racking my body until I'm spent. I crumple in my mother's arms and she gently rocks me, then she dries my face with the backs of her hands.

"I'll make you something to eat," she says, kissing my forehead and rubbing my cheeks. "We'll get through this together."

"You don't understand," I say.

She cups my face in her hands, then reaches around to my nightstand and sets the framed picture of Dad and Paige on my lap. "But I do understand, sweet girl. I understand completely. I've let the darkness of losing them consume me for too many years now. I won't lose you to that same darkness. We'll get through this, and we'll do it together. And besides, I promised Robert I would never let you slack one drop when it comes to your education, and I aim to keep that promise. Now go get a shower while I make us some breakfast."

I lock the door when I'm in the bathroom and slip off my clothes. I turn on the water, but I don't get in the shower. Instead, I open the medicine cabinet, staring at the old-fashioned razor that belonged to my dad. I gently lift it from the shelf and remove the blade inside it. I hold the blade to my wrist. If I muster the courage to make one deep slice, will I simply be reborn in another lifetime? Could reality be that I'm truly only one final heartbeat, one single breath, away from the only man I'll ever love?

Would this nightmare of living without Robert finally be over?

But when I recall the picture of Dad and Paige, I toss the blade into the trash bin and set my father's razor back in the cabinet. I'd never put my mother through the nightmare of losing me too. And Robert—my Robert deserves better than my self-pity. Deep down I know that, no matter how staggering the pain gets. He's spent lifetimes searching for me, loving me, missing me to the point of madness. And yet, he endured, strove to be a better man. He'd never forgive me for taking my own life, and I'd never expect him to. So somehow, some way, I'll get through this for him—be the woman he deserves.

And if the universe has one shred of kindness in her, she'll honor the oath I'm willing to make.

I step into the shower, warm water cleansing my aching body for the first time in several days. I look at the promise ring Robert placed on my finger just a few short weeks ago, at the two intertwined hearts etched on its surface.

And I make a few promises of my own.

CHAPTER 22

Summer, 2087

My breaths are shallow, but my nerves jar me into focus, force me to press on, no matter how tired I am. This task is too important not to finish. It's been so long since I've been here. A lifetime, actually. I think about the phrasing and smile. *A lifetime…*

Convincing the taxi driver to drop me off in the cemetery was no easy feat, but I suppose my power of persuasion's still intact, even at eighty-nine. I see the old oak and the angel statue that I know are near his final resting place. I'm grateful to spot them so quickly. My legs are like Jell-O, but I make my way toward his grave. *Soon, my love. Nearly there…*

When his headstone comes into view, I stop.

"Oh my darling," I mutter, overcome by the sight of a nineteen-year-old Robert smiling back at me from the small plaque with his image. It must've been added after the last time I visited. I touch his smiling face and trail a line around his honeyed curls. I trace along the words below his picture. *Robert Thomas Grafton, May 18, 1996— October 9, 2015. Beloved Son, Brother, and Friend. Love is Always*

Enough. I asked his mother to add the last line, although it didn't take much persuading. She knew me immediately from Robert's drawings, never doubted her son's past-life experiences in the slightest. Thank God for a mother's love, and belief, that one day her child would live again.

I realize that no one's been to visit Robert's grave for what looks like decades. But then again, who would there be? It's only me. I'm the last one. His parents have been dead for nearly thirty years, and even his baby brother's gone, not long after I buried my own mother. He was fifty-one. I think it was a heart attack. I haven't been back here myself in seventy-one years, simply because I know my Robert's spirit is not confined to the dirt and grass I'm standing on. No, there's never been a reason to pay homage to this place. He's much bigger than a burial plot. He's the air and sky around me, the star that's guided me into the wrinkles he so badly wanted to see on this tired, worn face. But I'm here now in this moment—minutes away from the completion of my pilgrimage through an existence without him, and it's precisely as it should be. I'm the one who had to do the searching this time, and in every way I knew how, I found him.

It takes the last bit of strength I possess to sit atop his grave, but I manage somehow. I'm comforted by the dozens of birds that are perched in the old oak just a few feet away, guarding his bones like little soldiers. Knowing that his final resting place has been filled with blue skies and birdsong gives me a peace I haven't felt in years. *Thank you* I mouth in their direction, my thoughts drifting to the tips of their wings, and the feathery plumes of their breasts. I place a hand on his headstone and with a shaky finger, retrace the lines forming his name.

"I'm here, my love. I like your birds." It's all I say at first, but there's much more to tell Robert. So much more to say… "I've missed you, my darling, to the point I almost couldn't bear it. And for so many years…"

I'm quiet for a couple minutes, mustering the strength

to say all the words that have remained unspoken. I've walked this earth for so long, fulfilling a destiny with quiet dignity, giving the universe what was required of me. My Robert sacrificed, tried with all he had to be a better man. Well, in the end, I had to be the woman who could honor that sacrifice, honor him, love him with all I had. And here at the end of this life, I delight in the fact that I did it, set things right. My Robert always thought he had to do more, had to love me more, had to find the missing piece to the puzzle that kept us "just a bit too little too late" in every lifetime. But the universe isn't as twisted as I always accused her of being. My true understanding of his sacrifice and devotion was the missing piece. But it is missing no longer…

I clear my tight throat and talk to my Robert. "When William took you from me, at first I wanted to die, too. I wasn't sure I had the strength to continue through this life without you. I'd spent a lifetime, up to that point, watching my mother grieve for my father and sister, and in my own way, I'd been grieving for you and our babies. But then you found me, and I was whole again. Having you ripped away crushed my soul, and I understood completely how you must've felt to have me stolen away from you, time and time again. When I got to the point that I felt I couldn't go on, I realized that living was exactly what I had to do. You'd spent every lifetime trying to be a better man, doing everything you could to get it right so the universe would allow us to be together. Well, I did the same thing, my love. To find you again, I went back to the only place I knew you would be…our wilderness.

"I used the scholarship money I earned from the Sunshine Warriors and attended college in Michigan. After graduating and working for several years, eventually I located the area where our cabin used to be, and purchased the land. I had my own cabin built there. It was like you were there with me, in every tree and blade of grass. And during the summer months, I'd travel to the river where we met. I swear when I was there, I felt your arms around me. Every time the wind tickled my neck, I recalled your lips and breath on my skin. And I realized in those moments, you were never far away. And guess what? I placed my music box in a metal case and buried it under our favorite rock along the river. You'll retrieve it again one day, my love, and this time, we'll unearth it together. I'll be right there by your side, I promise.

"Over the years I used the ancestry data you compiled on the kids to track down some of our surviving family members. I never told them who I really was, but it was nice to be a part of the lives our love created, even if it was in the simplest of ways. I even managed to acquire two pieces of furniture you'd made. One of them was my hope chest, and you were right, my love. It is indeed gorgeous. I have cherished it for thirty years. I surrounded myself with you in every way I knew how, and I was happy."

I pause to take a breath, realizing just how labored my breathing is becoming. But I'm close now. So close. Nearly done…

"In all the seventy-plus years I've been without you, there's never been another man. I now understand how you couldn't bring yourself to be with another girl after you lost me. We are our other halves, and I'm content with that. I have wrinkles on this face, just as you always desired, and I've earned them all. We both have. But I'm tired, my love. And now it's time."

I reach into the deep pocket of my dress and retrieve the silver rattle that belonged to our babies, along with a small, plastic container. I remove the remnants of silk flowers from a marble vase attached to Robert's headstone and drop the rattle inside it. I pour the contents of the container inside the vase as well. The plaster will conceal the rattle, hopefully keep it safe until the next life.

I manage to lie down atop the cool, granite slab, more tired than I've been in this life. My breaths are fading, but I don't fight it. I gaze at the heavens instead, shades of blue sky and puffy clouds soothing me. Soon, this tired body will be in the burial plot beside his, something I made sure of more than forty years ago. Love is indeed enough, and in the end it is all we take with us.

"We'll be together soon, my love. So very soon…"

I close my eyes to birdsong and the memory of his face.

CHAPTER 23

Spring, 2311

I step from the hoverpod and sit on the bench near Area 32. I set my bags in front of me and pull out my locator. They'll be here soon, but I still have at least ten minutes. Perfect. No way my surprise will be ruined now. I wish Robert could've been with me at my appointment this morning, but no one can be in two places at once. And his other task was equally important, but I'm nearly bursting to tell him the news.

I pull out my journal and touch the screen when it lights up. My parents gave it to me for my thirteenth birthday, the year before Robert and I reconnected in this lifetime. I set the date to September 19, 2299, and watch the screen as the video starts. It's the journal entry I made when Robert walked into my art class twelve years ago, and my world started spinning again…

"Robert," the teacher says, "you can take a seat anywhere you'd like."

I peek around the shoulders of the girl in front of me,

and my eyes connect with his. The smile I haven't seen in over two hundred years lights his face like a lantern, and every nerve ending in my body reacts to him. He's here. Finally. *We're together.*

He sits in the chair beside me at the back table and I don't hide the fact that I'm staring.

"Robert," I whisper.

He closes his eyes like my words give him life. "You…do you know me?"

"Yes," I reply, "with all my heart."

His relief is audible. "And what do you remember?"

I touch his hand. "*Everything.*"

"Oh, thank God." His eyes fill with tears. "My Anna…"

At that moment, we're the only two people in the room, on the planet, in the universe. He reaches under the table and takes my hand.

"You know," he says, "you're never getting rid of me again. Fate has spoken. We're bound to each other, forever."

"Forever," I agree.

He squeezes my hand tighter, his eyes never leaving my face.

I close the journal entry and the memory, but recall so many others that I see in my mind's eye. Some of the memories are weak, like flashing pictures faded in the backlight of darkness, just on the edge of day changing to night. But others are strong and clear, almost supernatural in their intensity: our wedding days, the births of our children, the first time I saw Robert along the river, the first time he took me in his arms and kissed me until I was breathless. I have loved this man for a thousand years, and I will love him for a million more.

"Mommy," I hear my sweet toddler say before I notice him and Robert headed toward me.

"Hey, little man. How you feeling, huh?" I scoop him into a hug and then sit him down on the bench beside me. I stand when Robert reaches me. "So, what did the pediatrician say?"

"He said he has an ear infection, prescribed some meds. He'll be fine."

Robert tugs me into a hug and places a hand on my growing stomach. "What I want to know is, how'd the ultrasound appointment go? Is it a boy or a girl?"

I reach slowly into my bag, wanting to savor the surprise I've had planned all morning. I pull out my music box and place it gently in his hands. "Well, let's just say we'll be needing this."

"It's a girl! I knew it!" I delight in his excitement as he picks up our son and hugs him close. "You're going to be a big brother, Michael. Mommy's having you a baby sister."

Robert includes me in the embrace and kisses me so tenderly that I fear my knees will buckle. His thumb trails my cheek and I close my eyes in the softness of my child's hand around my neck and Robert's around my waist.

"Oh, Anna, you make me so happy, do you know that? The absolute happiest man in the world."

"I do know it," I say, "with all my heart."

He's quiet for a few seconds, looking into my eyes so deeply, as if he's trying to pour his thoughts directly into my soul without any words at all. When he finally speaks, his words are simply, "Anna, all I am is loving you."

"Well, my darling, your love has always been enough."

We gather my bags and our small family and enter the next hoverpod as it approaches, hopeful for the future…for eternity…

For our forever.

ACKNOWLEDGEMENTS

I want to thank my husband, Joe; my children, Tim, Travis, Ben, and Austin; and my precious granddaughter, Lilliana Rose, for their faithful love and support. Without them, my life would be meaningless.

I also want to thank my parents, Chester and Sharon Collier, for teaching me that I can accomplish anything, and for their unwavering support of my passion for writing. I love you, Mama and Daddy.

I want to thank my sisters, my family, and my friends, especially my best friend, Joyce.

I want to thank Carrie, Sandi, and Candice for being beta readers and the best "write club" any girl could ask for.

I want to thank my fabulous cover artist, Najla, and my amazing editor, Rie.

And, lastly, I want to thank my Inkspell family, especially Melissa for believing in GLIMPSES, from the bottom of my heart.

ABOUT THE AUTHOR

Lee Ann Ward is an award-winning fiction author with a background in journalism and mass communications. She is also the former Senior Editor of a digital romance publisher. Her love of books started at the age of three, and she's been addicted ever since. She's published six novels (with her seventh and eighth on the way) and has written several more. When she's not writing, she's reading, singing, baking designer cakes, bowling and dreaming. She's married to Joe (who also happens to be her publicist) and they have 4 sons who they adore, and a granddaughter who is the love of their life. They make their home in the small fishing community of Bayou La Batre, Alabama.

You can find more on Lee Ann and her books at:

Author website: www.leeannward.com
Facebook: https://www.facebook.com/leeannwardbooks
Twitter: https://twitter.com/LeeAnnWard1115
Instagram: https://www.instagram.com/leeannward1115/
Goodreads:
https://www.goodreads.com/author/show/1275370.Lee_Ann_Ward

www.ingramcontent.com/pod-product-compliance
Lightning Source LLC
Chambersburg PA
CBHW022202170626
46807CB00005B/2313